S0-BMU-158

SILVER CREEK

SILVER CREEK

•

A.H. Holt

AVALON BOOKS
NEW YORK

WEST BEND LIBRARY

© Copyright 2003 by A.H. Holt
Library of Congress Catalog Card Number: 2002096669
ISBN 0-8034-9600-1
All rights reserved.
All the characters in this book are fictitious,
and any resemblance to actual persons,
living or dead, is purely coincidental.
Published by Thomas Bouregy & Co., Inc.
160 Madison Avenue, New York, NY 10016

PRINTED IN THE UNITED STATES OF AMERICA
ON ACID-FREE PAPER
BY HADDON CRAFTSMEN, BLOOMSBURG, PENNSYLVANIA

W
Hol

For my children:
Steve, Dale, Eric and Jamie,
and my sweetheart, Bobby Jess

Chapter One

John Garrett tied his gear behind his saddle and left the Wilson ranch just before daybreak. He followed the old Butterfield stage road northward for about thirty miles to the Rio Grande crossing just south of Mesilla. The first night on the trail he camped at Cooke's Spring.

His goal that morning was to reach the hills before the sun was high. He said his farewells to the ranch owner and the other cowboys the night before he left. Buck Wilson had wished him luck, and John had assured him that if he ever rode for another ranch, he would come back and ride for him. He didn't explain why he was leaving, he simply said he had business that needed tending and a long ride to get to where that business was. Wilson knew enough not to ask questions.

Garrett rode a long, rangy sorrel horse with the unlikely name of Prince. Sometimes he thought the name was kind of silly, but he had named the horse when he was a colt because he was almost too showy to be a working horse. He was still showy, as well as big and powerful, and he was the best trail horse John had ever owned. He lifted the reins and urged Prince to a mile-eating trot.

The second morning on the trail John broke camp early and rode two miles into Mesilla to stock up on supplies. There would be nights he would have to camp on the trail.

1

Later in the day, working his way northwest from Mesilla, he made good time. He was determined to save his horse's strength, so he stopped and made camp the second day after riding only twenty miles. He unsaddled Prince and rubbed him down thoroughly with his saddle blanket, then turned him loose to forage. There was little grass for him to find on the lower slopes of the Las Cruces Mountains.

"I have to take it easy and be patient," John said to himself. He desperately wanted to hurry, but he knew that pushing his horse too fast would be a foolhardy way to begin a journey of more than four hundred miles. A journey that would take him back to another life. A life he had sworn to forget.

Alec Gunnison's visit brought it all sweeping back. The anger, and the sickness he felt every time he thought of that last day. The day he left the ranch he loved and expected to live on for the rest of his life. He could still see Mason Garrett's angry face, and the whip in his left hand. Alec said he had a duty to go home and help his father in his trouble.

Well, John thought, *I'm going home, but only because it's my duty. When this is settled, I'll never stay.*

It was the best time of the year to travel. Most late afternoons John found water and a good place to camp. Whenever possible he stopped at a large ranch. The owner or foreman was sure to offer a meal and a bed in the bunkhouse for him and feed for his horse. Occasionally he spent the evening and night at a mining camp or a small town where he could get a hot meal.

When he passed the night in a town or at a ranch John always took time to groom Prince well and feed him grain at night. He repeated the process before they started out the next day. The big horse had great stamina, but he had been fed grain regularly and it would preserve his strength.

John followed the route he had taken when he left his home six years before. Remembering how he had burned with anger and bitterness as he rode away from all he loved was still painful. The anger had softened, but he was still bitter.

There was little in the way of a direct trail to follow in the direction he was traveling, but here and there a rough track had been marked by wagons. Those trails provided easy travel for a few miles until they turned in a different direction. It was late August and rains came almost every afternoon. The slopes of the White Mountains were covered in patches of green. This was the only time of year when there was color on the mountains southeast of Silver City.

John had turned north at a town called Deming that was once a stop for the Butterfield stage, then his route turned northwest, keeping the Mimbres River on his left. The going was easy near the river and he made the hundred miles to Silver City in only four days. This trail was once a favorite route of the Apache. The whole area was Apache territory. Ten years earlier no one would have been foolish enough to ride from Deming to Silver City alone. Only large well-armed groups were safe. But the Apache were gone. They had all been killed or tamed.

Leaving Silver City on a trail that led northwest to Buckhorn, John crossed a small river. It was probably a branch of the Gila. After that crossing his route turned more to the north and passed a short distance east of Mule Creek on an old trail into the Mogollons. It took several days for him to ride through the mountains. The valleys were covered in a thick growth of grama grass providing plentiful food for Prince. As the trail went upward, he passed through areas covered in scrub oak, and then reached forests of the tall, graceful ponderosa pine. Up higher, he could see aspens growing on southern slopes. Most nights he camped near a creek or spring that lay under large cottonwoods or willows. Game was plentiful. He often shot a rabbit from his horse's back and ended the day by enjoying it for his supper, roasted over his campfire.

When he finally crossed the San Francisco River and turned west toward Clay Springs John felt as though he had been on the trail a month, although he left the lake country and reached Clay Springs on his fourteenth day of travel. Clay Springs was a beautiful place to camp. After removing his gear and unsaddling the horse, he led Prince to a grassy area about a hundred yards from the spring. He had decided to stay at the spring for two full days to give the horse a rest. He had seen a small herd of deer less than a mile before he reached the spring, and wanted to try to get a shot at one.

At daybreak three days later John broke camp and set off to the northwest. His route would turn sharply back to the east before he reached the Tonto and then it would join a trail running northeast into the mountains.

Deep in the mountains, he decided to make a last stop at a little town that sat across the trail leading to an un-named river crossing. As he remembered, Ellison Grove wasn't much of a town, but it would surely have a mercantile with the supplies he needed. He looked forward to getting a meal someone else had cooked and a good night's rest in a bed for himself and a stable with a large bait of oats for Prince. He would be able to replenish his food supply, and buy more ammunition.

He felt sure he could reach the cabin in no more than two day's ride from Ellison Grove. He wanted to arrive alert and well rested. He hoped the cabin would be empty, but he knew there was no telling what he would find.

It was late afternoon when he rode into Ellison Grove. As he approached the town, he passed about a dozen scattered, shack-like houses and an unpainted church on his left. It was plain to see that the place was far from prosperous. The entire center of the town seemed to consist of one long block of buildings. The block was held down on the east by a large mercantile store and on the west by a livery stable. Some small shops and according to the fading sign, a combination saloon and hotel stood in between. John decided to stop first at the mercantile and get his supplies so he would be free to make an early start the next morning.

Tossing Prince's reins across the hitching rail, he dismounted and climbed the steps to the store porch. Four disreputable looking older men were sitting in chairs

propped against the front wall of the store. Each one nodded as he crossed to enter the double doors. The store clerk
was also an older man.

"How can I help you, mister?" the clerk said, examining
John with his eyes as he crossed to the counter.

"I need a few supplies." Without further conversation
John listed the supplies he needed. "I want five pounds of
flour, a pound of coffee, a quarter pound of salt, about five
pounds of bacon, and three cans each of beans and peaches.
I also want three boxes of .44s."

As the clerk rushed to fill his order John looked around
the store. It didn't look as though it was doing a booming
business. There weren't many things on the store shelves
except for the staple items such as food and various kinds
of ammunition. What little bit of stock there looked dusty
and neglected. So far the whole town of Ellison Grove
looked sort of run down. *I hope the hotel and saloon has
got a halfway decent bed and some food that tastes better
than jerky and water,* John thought.

Gathering his supplies into a cloth sack, John paid the
clerk and waited for change from a twenty-dollar gold
piece. The clerk examined the coin carefully then continued
to watch John's every move. The man seemed to want to
speak, but when he looked up at John's shuttered expression, he evidently decided questions would be unwelcome.
He finally just handed John his change and thanked him
for his business.

Under the intent stares of the four old men on the store
porch John stowed the boxes of shells in his saddlebags
and tied the bag of food supplies behind his saddle. Ignoring the men, he led his horse across the dusty street to the
hitching rack in front of the saloon. He intended to have a
meal and take a look at one of the rooms before he made
up his mind on whether to stay the night. He was beginning
to think he might be more comfortable if he moved on and
camped somewhere on the trail. The idea of staying in a
hotel that was part of a saloon, in a town that looked so
broke, was giving him an uneasy feeling in his stomach.

It was dim inside the saloon in the waning light of late afternoon. John stood in the doorway for a moment giving his eyes time to adjust. He saw a kid and an older man standing at the bar and five more men playing cards at a table nearby. The card players looked like cowboys. Aside from the man tending bar, the only other person he could see was a tired looking young woman standing at the foot of a set of steps that probably led to the hotel part of the establishment.

The place looked dangerous. John immediately decided to enjoy a glass of beer then hit the trail. He lost all appetite for trying the food advertised by a sign over the bar that was hand-lettered EATS. He caught the bartender's eye and ordered his beer. The man stopped talking, but continued to watch John with interest as he drew the beer and handed him the glass. John dropped a coin on the bar. Picking up the glass he walked to a table at the back of the room to sit with his back against the wall. Slowly sipping the cool beer, he began examining what he could see of each man in the room. He kept his hat brim pulled down enough to hide his eyes and slowly concentrated on each man.

He wasn't exactly sure what he was looking for, but he continued to sit sort of hunched over his glass as he examined the men. He was sure the saloon was a good place to stay ready for anything. He knew the men at the table were busy playing cards. One or the other would occasionally look toward the bar. He could hear the kid standing at the bar telling his companion how fast he could draw his gun. Suddenly, the kid turned and leaned back against the bar, looking across the saloon at John.

"Hey, stranger," he asked in a loud voice. "What are you hiding from?"

John kept his head down and ignored the question. Obviously irritated by John's silence, the young man continued. His voice was full of contempt. "You look like you might be on the run, fella. Is that why you're in Ellison Grove?"

The men at the card table began to look nervous. They

looked at each other for a moment. Without speaking they threw down their cards, picked up their money, and pushed back their chairs to stand. As the men moved toward the door to leave, the kid left the bar to come across the saloon and stand in front of John's table.

"Are you deaf, cowboy," he demanded belligerently, "or are you just too stupid to answer a question?"

John looked up into the rider's face. A closer look confirmed that the would-be bully wasn't much more than a boy. "Look, kid," he said quietly. "Go back over to the bar and mind your own business."

"You're my business right now," the boy's face contorted in anger as he answered. Stepping back from the table he dropped his right hand near his pistol. "You get on your feet and draw your gun or answer my questions, drifter."

John slowly stood, holding his hands up and away from his Colt. "Forget it, kid. I won't fight you. I don't shoot at children. Why don't you go on about your business and leave me alone."

"Are you too yellow to draw?" The boy snarled the words, his face red with anger.

"That must surely be my problem, son. You just run on home to your Mama now," John answered as he sat back down and picked up his glass, turning his head to take another sip of his beer. The boy sputtered with fury. There were witnesses in the saloon. He couldn't draw on a man who refused to fight back. He glared at John for a moment then turned and strode out of the saloon.

John sat very still and slowly finished his beer. When he stood up to leave he turned to check the man standing at the bar for any threatening movement. The bartender was busy polishing glasses and carefully ignored him. The man standing at the bar was busy looking into a glass of beer. John crossed to the saloon's double doors and stepped out onto the porch.

The boy from the saloon stood in the street beside Prince. He held John's Henry in his left hand. Raising the rifle high over his head, he yelled, "A man that won't fight don't deserve to have guns, yellow-belly!" As he finished speaking he threw John's rifle into the middle of the dusty street and lunged for his pistol with his right.

John drew and fired just as the young man began to raise his pistol. The boy dropped like a stone, his hat and gun falling under the horse's feet. At the sound of the shots men ran out of the saloon to gawk first at the fallen boy, then at John. One man turned and ran up the street, yelling for the sheriff. Grabbing his Henry out of the dust of the street, John picked up his horse's reins and started to mount up.

A tall, angry looking man who wore a sheriff's badge and carried a shotgun approached John. "You hold on there a minute, mister." The man John had noticed running up the street stood just behind the sheriff.

Staring at the face of the approaching man, John suddenly realized that he knew who this sheriff was. His name was Jake Thornton. He was a wanted outlaw in Texas, and a thoroughly dangerous man.

"The boy drew on me, Sheriff. I had no choice but to shoot."

"Who saw it happen?" The sheriff turned to the crowd that had gathered on the saloon porch. No one came forward. Although it was actually possible that no one had seen what happened. It was plain to John that no one was going to admit to having seen the fight even if they had.

"That's it, stranger," the sheriff said, stepping forward. "I'm locking you up until the circuit judge gets here. That's my sister's boy you gunned down. If he dies I'll see you hang for shooting him. He's nothing but a kid."

John knew he couldn't let this sheriff put him in jail. He didn't know a soul in this town and if there were no friendly witnesses to the gunfight, he wouldn't have a chance at a trial if the boy died. He knew he'd probably end up being shot trying to escape anyway with Jake Thornton as sheriff.

John was beginning to suspect that no matter what happened, the people of this town never intended for him to leave. For one thing, he had shown money at the mercantile when he bought his supplies and for another, he had a fine horse and outfit. His decision not to stay overnight in the place had been a good one, but he had to get out of Ellison Grove now.

Thornton stepped closer to John and lowering the shotgun, he raised his hand to reach out for his arm. John waited until the outlaw turned sheriff was in position, then hit him in the mouth with a stunning left, knocking him to the ground. As the man was falling, John reached his saddle in two jumps and dug his spurs in Prince's flanks as he turned him toward the western end of the town.

Lying as flat as possible against the horses neck, John urged him to a gallop as he settled in the saddle. The sound of scattered gunshots reached him as he passed the livery and turned onto the dusty road leading to the river. He guided the horse along the beaten track for a short distance, then turned off into some scattered trees and brush, slowing Prince to a smooth canter.

John stopped the horse as he topped a sharp rise and turned to look back. He expected to be followed, and he was not disappointed. Just as he turned, a group of ten or more men came around the livery barn, running their horses. He shook his head in disgust as he urged Prince over the little rise and turned west toward the mountains. Keeping the sorrel at a canter as long as the faint trail lasted, he slowed him to a trot as he entered an area strewn with rocks and full of places where the horse could easily break a leg if he put a foot wrong.

Twilight caught him well into the hills, back on a clear trail. As the darkness increased he had to slow his horse to a walk and let him find his own footing. The trail seemed to be heading down hill, and soon he noticed that the horse had picked up his pace. He was acting as though he smelled water.

"We must be coming to the river," John said aloud. "I

knew it wasn't too far. Maybe Thornton and his men will give up on me after we cross."

He shook his head and laughed aloud at his foolishness. He knew entertaining the idea that the men would just give up was foolish. The men were well behind him, but not nearly far enough for him to feel safe. Even if he kept moving all night the area he was riding through was so cut up and full of rocks and small canyons that he couldn't make much time. The sheriff or some of the local men riding with him probably knew the area well and they would be able to move much faster than he could.

Soon he could hear the river rushing along at the bottom of the deep cut in the rocks. As his horse picked his way down the narrow trail the sound grew to a roar. Suddenly the big horse stopped and John could see the water. It was almost black in the meager light and looked menacing.

He dismounted and let the horse drink a little. Pulling Prince back from the water, so he wouldn't drink too much too quickly, John knelt at the edge of the water to refill his canteen and quench his own thirst. He sat down beside the water and rested, waiting patiently. The posse was gaining on him while he waited, but he had to let his horse drink again if he was going to carry him to safety.

After a few minutes, John let Prince take a longer drink then he climbed back into the saddle. He knew that trying to cross the river when it was so dark in the canyon that he couldn't see the rocks on the other bank was foolhardy at best, but he couldn't stay where he was. He'd be caught and shot or more likely, he'd be hanged out of hand, if he had Thornton figured right.

Guessing that the landing on the other side would be roughly straight across from where he entered the river, he put the sorrel into the water, heading him up-stream to swim against the rushing current. He was hoping that if he missed the low place on the other bank in the dark, he would be a little up-stream, so he could still reach safety before he was swept away by the swift water. Luck and the sheer power of the big sorrel horse helped him guide Prince to a spot where he could climb out of the river and back up on the trail.

The track away from the river led sharply upward. The rocky wall on this side was almost straight up so that the narrow path followed a series of cutbacks zigzagging to the top. John had almost reached level ground when Thornton and several of his men rode into the cut on the other side of the canyon.

He heard the men shouting when they spotted him in the dim light of the rising moon. Bullets immediately began to hit the rocks around John. He was within easy rifle range. The only thing that was saving him from the wild barrage of firing was that the men were riding downhill and the movement of their horses ruined their aim. He knew that it wouldn't be long before one of them stopped and dismounted in order to get a good shot. He wouldn't have a chance as long as he was in such an exposed position.

Just as the straining horse reached the top of the canyon and leaped for the open, a bullet smashed into John's back, high up on his right shoulder. He grabbed for the horse's mane with his left hand as his head swam with shock and pain. He almost lost consciousness. Unguided, the horse slowed, but kept moving. John lay his head against Prince's neck and twisted one hand in his mane to keep himself from falling. He shook his head to clear it.

After a few minutes, the shock began to wear off enough so he could think. He knew he had to keep moving, and pray that the wound didn't leave enough blood on the ground to make a trail for the men following him. No, he couldn't just keep on riding. He would have to stop and bind the wound to stop the bleeding if he were going to have any hope of getting away.

He slowed his horse to a walk and turned away from the trail. Urging his horse into a thicket of scrubby oak trees, he stopped. Moving as though in a dream, John opened his left hand and released his grip on the horse's mane. He pushed against the horn of his saddle until he could sit erect. The pain seemed to envelop his entire body. He was breathing hard with the effort it took to stay upright in the saddle. He felt weak and dizzy. Using his left hand, he rummaged in his saddlebag for a spare shirt. He draped the shirt over his right shoulder with most of it covering the gaping wound created by the bullet's exit. Pulling the shirt as tight as he could, he tied the sleeves in a knot to hold it in place.

"Blast," he muttered, "that probably won't do much good." It was the best he could do though, with only his teeth and one hand.

The dizziness John felt when the bullet first hit him was beginning to subside. He felt strong enough to keep riding. He had to keep on riding. He held the horse to a walk through the brush, guiding him carefully to avoid open spaces where he would leave tracks. He didn't need to make it easy for the posse to follow. He was so thirsty, he had to drink, and he had to find more water before he emptied his canteen.

John began to worry about his horse. He wondered how much longer the big sorrel could keep on going without rest. Maybe Alec would ride out to meet him. Then he remembered that Alec wouldn't be there. Alec went to California. It felt like he was getting close to the cabin. He shook his head to clear it. His thinking was getting muddled.

Jerking his head up, John suddenly realized his horse had stopped to graze. He turned to look behind him. He could see the horse had wandered well away from the trail. They were in the edge of a thick pine forest. The land rose sharply to the north, so he would be climbing if he kept on in the direction he was headed. Was he headed in the right direction? Would he be able to hang on as weak as he was? Unsure exactly where he was, John was aware enough to know it would be harder for the posse to find him if he continued deeper into the wood.

He pulled up on the reins to stop the sorrel from grazing and nudged him farther under the trees. Limbs brushed against him. He was so weak it felt as though the trees were deliberately trying to knock him out of the saddle. Finally the tired horse stopped to graze again in a small clearing. The sun was shining. John could feel warmth on his back. He was so thirsty. He reached for his canteen then remembered it was empty. He felt a wave of dizziness pushing his head back down against the horse's neck. He was so tired—so thirsty.

Chapter Two

Stepping down from the saddle, the tall girl led the black mustang back into the rocks far enough not to be easily seen from the road and dropped his reins to ground tie him. She had reached the northern slope early this morning and decided it would be a good time to climb over the rim and check for tracks. She was in an area near the main road where it curved within two miles of Silver Creek ranch. Bushwhackers had been sneaking into the valley by some hidden route; perhaps she could find where they had come down through the pines.

Andrea Blaine climbed up in the rocks to sit in a spot between a group of boulders where she could watch the winding road below. After about ten minutes, she started suddenly and jumped down to run to her horse and pulled a small brass telescope out of her saddlebag. Climbing back up on the rocks, she sighted over the ridge at a place where the road entered a wooded area and curved out of sight.

A sorrel horse was trotting along the dusty track. It wore a Spanish saddle and bridle with a lot of silver. The reins appeared to be tied to the saddle horn. The horse held to a steady gait, moving along the middle of the road as though he had a definite destination. Even from this distance she could see that the horse was big. His body was long and rangy and he moved with a beautiful, fluid stride.

The girl watched the horse for a moment then snapped the glass shut and hurried back to her pony. Returning the glass to her saddlebag, she jumped in the saddle. The pony responded immediately to the pressure of her knee on his side and bounded down the hill, following a path that curved around the rocks. When they reached the open, Andrea urged him to a canter and reached the road ahead of the rider-less horse.

Dismounting in the middle of the road, Andrea stood quietly, examining the sorrel as he approached. The big horse slowed to a walk and stopped a short distance away from her. His head was held high and his ears were erect. He eyed her balefully, not sure whether to trust her. His nostrils were quivering and he lifted both his front feet a couple of times.

The girl held out one hand. "Come here boy," she said. Her voice was soft and gentle. "Come on, I won't hurt you."

The horse nickered as though greeting her and took a step forward. He lowered his head slowly and placed his soft nose in the girl's outstretched hand. "There's a good boy," she murmured, rubbing his nose. "What in the world are you doing trotting along here with no rider?"

Andrea patted the sorrel's neck and worked her way around to his side to examine the big Spanish saddle. There was a bedroll and a bag of supplies tied behind the saddle and a business-like Henry rifle was in a sheath. A dark stain on the saddle was dry, but it smelled like blood. She stood still beside the horse for a few minutes, puzzling over the situation.

"Somebody was riding you, weren't they, big boy," she said. "I wonder where he is, and what happened to him?" It was obvious that the horse didn't just stray. No one who cared for a horse would leave his reins tied like that, and the condition of this horses' gear and his hooves and smooth, shiny coat made it plain that he was well cared for.

Finally the girl decided that she had to find out what

happened to the horses' rider. Catching up her pony's reins, she jumped back into her saddle. Holding the sorrel's reins in her left hand, she continued to talk to reassure him.

"Come on with me, Beauty. We'll follow your tracks and see if we can find out where you lost your rider." She gave a little pull on the reins as she spoke and the horse turned and followed her willingly. The big sorrel was obviously used to people and unafraid. His back trail was plain and easy to follow. Each track was clearly outlined in the dust of the road.

As they reached the end of the plateau and the road entered the woods, the sorrel pushed ahead of Andrea's pony, easily yanking the reins from her hand. He turned away from the road and went directly into the woods. The slight path he followed led them straight down hill and deep into the pines. The horse had left no tracks to provide a back trail under the pines because the floor of the forest was covered in a thick bed of pine needles. Andrea guided her pony along behind the sorrel, wondering how far he was leading them. The sorrel picked up his pace as they neared an opening in the trees, then trotted into the small circle of sunshine and stopped to nose the side of a man lying on the ground.

Andrea slipped off her pony and ran to the man. Suddenly cautious she stopped before she got within reach and inspected the man carefully. She turned to look around the edges of the little glen to make sure no one else was there. At the same time, she took a small handgun out of her jacket pocket and held it ready.

The man was lying flat on his back with his arms spread straight out from his sides. He looked dead. Once she had convinced herself the man was alone, Andrea knelt beside him and placed one hand on his chest. He was breathing. His face was pale and his eyes were closed. His shirt felt wet to Andrea's hand. There was blood soaking through the cloth. She pulled open his unbuttoned shirt to reveal a thick, blood-soaked bandage.

"Oh, my Lord, he's been shot."

The man opened his eyes at the sound of her voice, and groaned. He stared up at Andrea blankly. His eyes were light, but the pupils were large and dark with pain.

"Get me some water, son," he whispered.

Putting her pistol back in her pocket, Andrea ran to her pony and untied her canteen from the saddle. Rushing back to kneel beside the man again, she slid her arm under his uninjured shoulder. "Here mister, let me help you raise your head." Lifting the man's head up a little so he could drink, she held the canteen to his lips.

"More."

The man's weight became too much for Andrea's arm and he slipped back to the ground. He was almost fainting again.

"I'll give you some more water in a minute, mister. I've got to stop that wound from bleeding." Andrea pulled the man's shirt away from his left shoulder. The bandage had been clumsily tied and had worked itself loose.

"Gosh, you must have bandaged this yourself," she said. "Do you have anything in your pack I can use to tie this up properly?"

Struggling to stay conscious, John whispered, "There's another shirt in my saddle bag."

Andrea found the shirt and tore it into strips. She removed the soggy bandage. It had covered a nasty wound high up on the man's shoulder. She struggled to raise the man enough to look at the place on his back where the bullet entered. That wound was about the size of a man's little finger. Its edges were swollen and blue looking.

"You were shot in the back," she exclaimed.

The man didn't answer. He was limp and his eyes were closed. He had fainted again. Andrea hurriedly made a thick pad to place over the jagged wound left by the bullets' exit and drew the bandages as tightly as she could, turning him so she could pull them across his chest and over his shoulder. When she had done all she could to stop the wound from bleeding she sat down on the grass beside the unconscious man and tried to imagine what could have happened. It was almost noon when the man stirred again. He moaned as he reached for the bandage, then he opened his eyes.

John could feel the sun on his face. He was in a clearing. As his vision cleared he saw the boy sitting cross-legged a few feet from him. He looked to be about fourteen or fifteen years old. He was dressed in rough riding pants and a light jacket. A wide-brimmed hat was pushed back on his head to reveal a smooth, tanned face and green eyes. His features were well cut and refined looking. His slim brown hands were idly braiding blades of grass.

John touched the thick bandage around his shoulder. *That kid must have put a real bandage on my shoulder.* The pain had eased some, but he was as weak as a kitten. His whole body screamed for water.

"I'm thirsty," he whispered.

"Oh good, you're awake. Here let me help you drink." Andrea said as she moved closer and leaned forward to lift his head and hold a canteen to his lips. "You're thirsty from losing so much blood, mister. You're lucky to be alive."

"What's your name boy?" the man asked after he drank.

"I'm Andy Blaine. What's your name?"

John struggled to a sitting position. He stared at the boy for a moment, trying to think what to say. Finally, he answered. "My name is Kyle Turner. Have you got any food, son?"

"I've got some biscuits. Hold on a minute." Andrea ran to her pony and pulled a small package wrapped in a kerchief out of her saddlebag.

John accepted the food eagerly. "Thank you, son. It was early yesterday when I last ate."

"Are you on the dodge, Mr. Turner?"

John studied the youth's face. His brilliant green eyes were full of concern and curiosity.

"In a way I guess I am. I was headed for that old cabin on Silver Creek."

"How'd you know about that cabin? Are you from around here?"

"Someone told me about it. I thought I could hole up there until I got my strength back."

"It's still a good four miles or more to Silver Creek. You can't ride that far with that shoulder."

"I'll have to ride that far. I sure can't lie out here in the open. Will you help me get there?"

John watched several changes of expression cross the boy's face. He looked at first perplexed, then he finally looked determined. "I don't know as I ought to, but I guess I couldn't leave you here in the open. You being helpless like you are now," the boy said. "The cabin at Silver Creek isn't far from my home. I'll help you get there and then I can bring my mother to tend your shoulder."

"No," John said, shaking his head. "No, son. I don't want anyone else to know where I am. The guy who shot me might come looking for me and asking questions. If no one else knows where I am, no one can give me away."

Andrea stared at the man for a moment. He looked like he could be an outlaw. His clothes had seen rough wear. His black hair was too long and most of his face was covered in dark whiskers. The only things he had that looked well cared for were his guns and the big sorrel horse. She finally decided that none of that mattered. Whatever the man had done, he was too weak for her to leave him lying out in the woods without food or water.

"I'll help you, Mr. Turner. I ride every day. I can bring you some food and look after your wound until you can get around enough to defend yourself."

"I'm obliged to you, son. Can you catch my horse?"

"I think so. He came right up to me on the road. What's his name?"

"I call him Prince. It seems to sound kind of silly now, but he was such a pretty colt he seemed to need a fancy name."

"He's a beauty all right." Andrea walked across the clearing and called to the horse.

"Prince, come here, boy." The horse willingly allowed himself to be caught and followed Andrea to John's side.

John was still sitting up, but his head was feeling light from loss of blood. His shoulder was on fire. He reached up to catch a stirrup with his left hand and pulled himself unsteadily to his feet. With Andrea's help he was finally able to struggle into the saddle.

"God, I'm weak," he muttered to himself. Turning to Andrea he asked, "How far did you say that cabin was?"

"It's at least four miles straight east through the woods. You sure don't want to go around by the road. It's easier going, but it's not only more than two times as far, someone will come along and see you for sure."

John couldn't answer. He was busy gritting his teeth to keep from groaning out loud. The pain was bad. He had to hold on to the saddle horn with his good hand to keep from falling off the horse. When he finally got his breath enough to speak, he said, "You go on ahead, boy. Prince will follow your pony."

Andrea mounted her horse and turned him into the woods. John nudged Prince with his knees and fell in behind the pony.

As she led the way into the thick pines Andrea thought about this strange day. She had started out from the ranch house that morning before dawn. She reached the pines at first light. Then she had gradually worked her way over the hills to that sheltered valley on the northwest side until she came to the track that led up to the large, flat boulder overlooking the road. That was where she had first seen the sorrel horse.

Dressed in her usual faded jeans and oversized jacket, with her hair tucked under her hat, she looked like a young boy. It was her favorite outfit for riding and working around the ranch. It was no wonder this stranger assumed she was a boy. Her clothes, combined with her name, had earned her the nickname "Andy." It was what her father, her brother, and the Silver Creek riders always called her.

Andrea loved working and riding with her father's cowboys. They treated her as an adored little sister. She had spent every hour possible in the woods since she was old enough to ride alone and was a crack shot with her rifle. She provided most of the game needed for the family table and for the bunkhouse cook. No one knew the hills and forests around Silver Creek the way she did. She seemed to lead the way through the thick pines on a trail she knew by instinct.

Heading southwest, and gradually moving down and across the hillside, she kept the horses under the shelter of the huge pines. The thick carpet of needles covering the ground would hide their tracks. She knew that even if someone followed the wounded man's trail to the spot where he fell off his horse he would be safe now, because they wouldn't be able to follow their tracks through the forest.

The ride was a nightmare for John. He clung to the saddle horn with his good hand, gritting his teeth against the pain in his shoulder. It felt as though every step the horse took caused a pain to shoot through his shoulder and arm. Sweat poured down his face and soaked what was left of his shirt.

"I'm probably bleeding again," he muttered as he felt a clinging blackness closing in. Shaking his head to stop the buzzing, he kept his seat in the saddle by pure determination.

The boy's voice seemed to come from far away. "Here's the cabin, Mr. Turner. Can you get down?"

John struggled to open his eyes. Andrea was standing at his knee. He was too exhausted to speak. He placed his left hand on Andrea's shoulder and slipped out of the saddle, never noticing that his weight nearly made her knees buckle. He had to hold on to the saddle to keep from falling. Andrea supported him as much as she could as he struggled to walk the few steps from the horse's side to the door of the cabin.

As she pushed the door open, it was easy to see that the cabin was empty and unused. It was still furnished with a table, two chairs, and a built-in bunk. A water bucket, a shovel and several other rusty tools were piled in one corner. The room smelled musty from disuse.

"Nobody's been here for a long time," Andrea said. "I'll take the blanket off that bunk and go get your bedroll, it'll be cleaner. Here, sit down on the bunk while I hobble your horse and bring in your gear." Tossing the dusty blanket in the corner, she left the cabin, grabbing up the wooden water bucket as she went out the door.

Feeling weak and sick, John leaned back on the bare mattress of the bunk. He couldn't see any fresh blood on the bandage. The boy did a good job of bandaging, he thought. He ran his hand over the heavy bandages. They felt dry.

"Thank God," he muttered. "If I don't get any infection I should be all right in a few days."

He felt for his pistol and settled it in place against his thigh. He was in no shape to defend him self. There was no reason for anyone to connect him with this place. He was aware enough to know that Thornton and the posse wouldn't be able to follow his tracks through the pine forest.

As his head cleared, John remembered that it was a lucky shot that had hit his shoulder. He had almost reached the shelter of the rocks above the river. After he was wounded, he remembered holding on to Prince's mane to keep from falling out of the saddle. He had been in and out of reality ever since. When he had finally made it into some trees and was sure he had lost Thornton and his crew, he was a couple of miles below Eagle Rock. Then he had doubled back across the river. He felt sure the posse would never even try to track him this far.

It took two trips for Andrea to get John's saddle and other gear into the cabin. She brought a bucket of fresh water in the cabin and placed it on the floor within John's reach. Somewhere she had found a gourd dipper and she put it in the bucket so John could easily get a drink when he needed it.

"I hobbled your horse in a open place to the north of the

cabin, up near the spring. He'll have plenty of water and grass. He'll be hard to see where he is unless someone happens to come right up into the clearing."

She walked over to the bunk and covered John with the blanket from his bedroll. "I've got to hustle on home, Mr. Turner," she said. "My mother will be fit to be tied as it is. I usually get back to the house much earlier than this. I'll come back up here a little after dark tonight and bring you some food and something to clean your wound properly. I'll change that makeshift bandage for you then. You rest and keep still so your wound can close."

John opened his eyes to watch the boy leave the cabin. Almost asleep, he could tell the boy was speaking, but he couldn't understood what he was saying.

Andrea ran to her pony and jumped in the saddle. She followed a faint path through the woods, and turned toward home. The cabin was high above the ranch, hidden in heavy pines. It was nearly a mile down a narrow path to where the valley opened up. The trail was so rough it wasn't safe to let the pony go much faster than a walk. When she reached the valley floor she urged the pony to a run.

As soon as she reached the level the open range spread out for miles. Silver Creek meandered lazily, crossing the range three times to carry the precious water that made the valley so rich. Andrea's father had purchased the ranch from Alec Gunnison, the old man who had lived in the cabin at the headwaters of the creek. The same cabin that the wounded man was hiding in.

Russ Blaine had built the Silver Creek ranch house himself. He dragged the great logs down from the hills with a team of three mules. He raised the walls with a block and fall and the help of his son Bill and Sandy Miller, a rider who was now serving as his ranch foreman. The big house was long and low, with a wide porch running across the front and back. He had shipped in large windows at great expense to open the front of the house to the spectacular view across the valley to the surrounding hills.

When she reached the barn, Andrea unsaddled her pony and turned him into his stall. She stopped to thoroughly wipe him down with his saddle blanket, then fed him a generous scoop of oats, and made sure he had plenty of hay. As soon as he was settled she hurried toward the house. The horse was free to go out into the corral to get water after he finished eating.

"Andrea? Is that you?" Julie Blaine called as she stepped out of the back door on to the porch.

Uh-oh, Andrea thought. *I'm in for it now.* She shook her head. Her mother always called her by her full name when she was displeased with her, refusing to use the masculine nickname "Andy" her daughter preferred.

As Andrea stepped up onto the back porch her father came to the kitchen door to stand beside his wife. "Where have you been, girl?" he yelled, sounding angry. "Your mother's been having a fit. You should have been here hours ago."

Standing in the doorway with his hands on his hips, Russ Blaine was a formidable figure. He had a few specks of gray in the sides of his black hair and plenty of wrinkles in his sun-baked face, but he was still built like a lumberjack. Most people cringed when he raised his voice to them.

Andy smiled and reached out to pat his right arm as she came up beside him. "I'm sorry to worry you, Daddy, I forgot the time."

Smiling down at her, Blaine said, "Well hurry and wash up, honey. Supper's almost ready. You should have been here to help get the meal, Andy. You know your mother needs you."

"I'll clean up after we eat, Daddy. Please don't fuss." Ignoring her mother's stern face she poured cold water from a bucket into the enamel wash basin on the long bench near the back door and washed her face and hands. Still looking down, she dried on the rough towel hanging on a nail above the basin. Julie Blaine made a sound of disgust and whirled to leave the doorway. Andrea smiled at her father as she slipped past him into the kitchen.

"Hey, Mama," said Andrea crossing the room to the dish safe. "I'm sorry I'm so late. I'll set the table."

"Andrea Blaine, you worry me sick roaming around on that pony like a wild Indian."

Julie Blaine was tall and slim like her daughter. She had the same golden-brown curls and glittering green eyes. She stood near the big iron stove with her hands on her hips. Her expressions alternated between anger, concern, frustration, and pride in her beautiful young daughter.

"Andrea, I'm going to ask your father not to allow you to ride anymore if you can't come home when you say you will. Anything could happen to you and we would never even know. It's not decent for a young woman to be out riding around the woods alone like you do."

"Aw, Mama. I'm perfectly safe."

"Oh, really?" Suppose you would happen on that Rafe Willis or some of his riders? He knows you're a girl."

"I'm careful, Mama, and my pony can outrun any other horse around here." Andrea couldn't help thinking of the big red sorrel Kyle Turner rode. He sure looked like he could run.

Mother and daughter worked quickly and the meal was soon prepared. Andrea called her father to the table. As Blaine entered the kitchen she looked up and asked, "Where's Billy, Daddy? Is he home?"

"Lord only knows where that boy is, honey. He ain't come back from town yet. I'm beginning to worry about him myself."

Andrea felt the fear she always experienced when her brother stayed away from home like this. He was probably drinking with some of his cronies over in Hinton. He had made friends with a group of rough boys when they first moved to Arizona and as they got older their wildness seemed to grow worse and worse. Blaine kept his son busy on the ranch and out of trouble most of the time, but it had gotten hard for him to control a twenty-year-old. Andrea was certain her brother was set for serious trouble if he kept hanging around with his childhood buddies.

"I sure hope he gets back tonight," she said, hiding her concern. "He promised to bring me some dress goods."

Russ Blaine laughed loudly. "What do you want with dresses?" You've been running around dressed like a boy for so long most people have forgotten we ever had a girl."

"Oh, Daddy. That's not funny. If I dressed like a girl I'd be trapped here in the house. You know that."

"That's where you belong, Andrea," her mother said emphatically. "You're going to be eighteen soon, you can't go on like this forever."

"I know, Mama. But we don't have enough riders to patrol the whole valley. I know the woods better than any of the men do and Daddy needs my help. Someone has to keep watch and I'm the logical one. You know I'm as safe out there as I would be right here in the house."

"Well, it's just not ladylike. My mother would have fainted at the sight of you in those disreputable looking pants."

"Most western girls wear pants now, Julie." Russ Blaine reached across the table to pat his wife's hand. "Let the girl alone. She's a better guard than some of the men, and I need her help."

"By the way, Daddy," said Andrea, "I saw Burt Stilwell and Whitey meet someone near the slope up to the rim just after dawn this morning. They were close to the path that leads up by Glade Springs and over to Hostetter's old place. It was no more than an hour after I left the house. It couldn't have been past six o'clock."

"Burt and Whitey meeting someone?" Blaine looked worried. "Could you tell who it was?"

"No, I couldn't tell who the rider was. I was too far away. I recognized our riders by their horses. Whoever it was they met was waiting up there for them. Which makes me think he camped right there or somewhere nearby last night. Our hands rode up to those big sycamores near the path and set their saddles like they were waiting for something. It wasn't long before the rider came out of the woods. He was on foot and leading his horse. Burt and

Whitey dismounted and stayed there talking to him for about ten minutes, then they got back on their horses and rode back down to the herd."

"As soon as Burt and Whitey left the other man got right on his horse and rode on up past the spring and over the rim. His horse was a small gray mustang. I've never seen it before."

Looking astonished Blaine thought a minute before he replied. "I don't know anyone who rides a gray horse except that big dapple-gray old Garrett rides."

"I know it wasn't Mason Garrett. The horse was way too small to be his and the man was slim and much shorter."

"You can bet I'm going out to the bunkhouse after supper. Burt and Whitey have darn sure got some tall explaining to do." Blaine still looked shocked and puzzled, but he also looked angry.

Andrea got up from the table and started to gather up the plates and utensils. "I'm going right to bed after I help Mama clean up," she said. "My bed will sure feel good. I rode farther than I usually do today and I'm tired."

"I'll say good night then," her father said as grabbed his hat and he went out the back door. "I'll see you at breakfast."

Andrea hurried through washing the dishes. When the kitchen was clean and neat again, she kissed her mother good night, went into her room and closed the door. Julie Blaine removed her apron and went out to the front porch. Russ would join her there when he came back from the bunkhouse. It was a ritual with them. They sat there on the porch together for an hour or more almost every evening when the weather permitted. They always talked over the events of the day, while her father relaxed and smoked a pipe.

It wasn't long before Andrea heard her father's footsteps on the front porch floor. Her room was at the back of the house off the kitchen, but with the door cracked she could hear him clearly.

"Did you talk to the men, Russ?" her mother asked.

"I couldn't, those boys are taking night turn guarding the herd. That's why they were out so early this morning. I'll just have to wait until tomorrow and ride out there. I reckon I can wait until then to find out what's going on."

Andrea listened to her parents' voices for a moment. She could tell by the creaking sounds she heard when her father settled back in his big chair. She guessed it would take a half an hour or more for him to smoke his pipe. She'd have ample time to get some food and other supplies together and carry the pack out to the barn before her parents came back in the house to go to bed.

Moving carefully to avoid making noise, Andrea let herself out of her room and shut the door. She tiptoed across the kitchen to wrap several biscuits and some meat left over from supper in a clean cloth. Almost holding her breath for fear of dropping something, she opened cupboards and gathered up bacon and coffee and other things she thought the rider would need. When she had found all the things she could think of to take she carried the heavy pack to her room.

After looking over what she had lying on the bed, Andrea slipped out of her room again and got a bottle of whiskey and a clean shirt from her father's wardrobe. Finally, she added a wool blanket, a towel, several candles, and some clean rags from the linen cabinet to her collection.

"Mr. Turner will surely think I'm not coming at all if I don't hurry," Andrea muttered aloud. She carefully pushed both of her pillows down under her quilt so it would look like she was sleeping if her mother or father should happen to open the door to her room. Then she went to the window at the back of the house facing the barn and corrals and peeped out. It was full dark. If she hurried she could climb out of the window and get across the back yard and past the bunkhouse before moonrise. It might be kind of difficult to explain what she was doing if someone caught her sneaking out to the barn carrying a large bundle wrapped in a blue blanket.

Easing the window up, Andrea leaned out over the windowsill, dropped the pack on the ground, and scrambled out after it. As soon as her feet hit the ground, she grabbed the pack with both hands and walked quickly to the barn. Lights were still on in the bunkhouse. Andrea moved as quietly as possible when she passed the building, keeping in the shadow of the trees at the back of the yard. She could hear the men talking through the open windows.

When she reached the barn, she went directly to her pony's stall and spoke to him softly, "Easy, easy now, Pat. We're going for a ride." She smoothed his blanket, and threw the saddle on his back. She found a piece of rawhide to tie the pack to the horn so she could hold it steady as she rode. Leading the pony, Andrea walked through the back door of the barn and into the edge of the woods. She knew that if she went straight out beside the house the way she normally rode her parents would be sure to see her. She continued to walk and lead her horse for a few hundred yards from the bunkhouse before she mounted. As soon as she was far enough away from the buildings not to be heard, she mounted and put the pony to a trot.

As she rode across the valley, Andrea puzzled over her strange reaction to Kyle Turner. Her father, brother, and their riders had been fighting off cattle thieves and men who wanted to force them out of Silver Creek for almost two years. This valley had the best water for miles around, so other cattlemen wanted it. The creek was spring fed, and the water level never ran low. Under the circumstances, she knew she should have been afraid of a stranger, especially one who confessed to being wounded while being chased by a posse, and she certainly knew she should tell her father about him. *No,* she thought, *I can't do that. The man is too weak and helpless to betray.*

Finally she convinced herself that if the man were any threat to her father she would find that out while he was recovering from the bullet wound. He had accepted her as a boy. That would make her safer. She could help him and possibly she could find out how he knew about the old cabin, and why he had been traveling to Silver Creek.

When Andrea entered the dark cabin she could see the outline of the rider lying across the bunk where she had left him. His voice startled her as she walked across the room to place the heavy pack on the table. "I heard your horse," he murmured weakly. "I'm glad to see you."

Andrea went over to kneel beside the bunk and check the bandage on his shoulder. It was still dry. "How do you feel?" she asked.

"I'm weak and tired. I'm so thirsty. I drank all of the water you left."

"That's natural after you lost so much blood. I'll get another bucket of water and then I'll clean that wound and re-bandage it." She grabbed the bucket and ran out of the cabin to walk up the path to the spring. The big sorrel horse snorted a greeting as she entered the clearing.

When she returned with the fresh water, John had pushed himself to a sitting position on the edge of the bunk. "Help me to the table," he said. He caught Andrea's shoulder with his left hand and pulled himself to his feet. She gritted her teeth as she felt his weight. He was taller than her father was and almost as big.

"You shouldn't try to get up," Andrea said. "You should have stayed where you were. I could re-bandage your shoulder without you moving."

"Oh, God, it hurts. I may pass out again when you pull that bandage off, but I have to move, I can't give in to this."

"Don't worry, if the bandage is stuck I'll soak it off. I've seen my mother do it for one of our riders." Andrea untied the blue blanket and took out some of the clean rags and the bottle of whiskey. She placed them on the rough table and lit a candle.

"I'll need to clean your wound with this whiskey. It should be cleaned with carbolic, I know, but Mother keeps her medicine box in her room and I couldn't get to it with-out getting caught."

John reached for the whiskey bottle with his left hand and downed several big swallows. "You're a good kid. I'm beholden to you, son." His gray eyes closed against the pain in his shoulder.

Andrea dropped her head to hide a smile and pulled most of the rough bandage from his chest and his shoulder. "This doesn't look wet. That's good. If the wound has closed and you don't have any fever you'll get better fast."

"It'll take weeks for me to get my full strength back. I lost a lot of blood. I couldn't stop to tie it up properly."

Andrea studied John's face for a moment. "You were running away from someone when you were shot?" Embarrassed to pry, she turned to pick up the water bucket and place it on the table to hide her face.

John watched Andy's slim figure bend to get something else from the pack. He was virtually helpless. He would have to put his trust in this youngster if he were going to survive. He thought he could explain the circumstances that had brought him here without telling the boy too much. He had to find out more about what was happening at the Double G and on Silver Creek before he told anyone who he was or revealed all his reasons for coming here.

Andrea soaked one of the rags in the cold water and placed it over the loosened bandage. "I brought biscuits and beef for your supper. It's a shame it's all gone cold, but I'm afraid to light a fire to heat it up. Thank goodness the weather is mild. The smoke from a fire would bring my father's men running up here."

"I can do without a fire for a while, and biscuits and beef sound wonderful even if they are cold."

As Andrea opened the bundle of food and placed it on the table before him, John asked, "How long has your family lived here?"

"My father bought old Alec Gunnison's patent about five years ago. Daddy moved us out here because our doctor told him that Mother's lungs were weak and she would develop consumption if he didn't take her to a drier climate.

He recommended the Arizona Mountains so Daddy sold our place in Georgia and we just packed up and moved."

"Daddy met Alec Gunnison over in Flagstaff. The old man was looking for a buyer for the valley. He said he was bothered with rheumatism and wanted to go to California where the weather was warm all year. People we met in Hinton told us later that there were several other people in town who wanted to buy the place, but Gunnison wouldn't sell to them. He never did tell us his reasons. We've only learned the full story in the last few years."

"What do you mean, the full story?" John asked as he watched Andrea working on his shoulder. Her sleeves were rolled up to expose rounded white arms. Her slim brown hands moved deftly and her touch was gentle.

"There's a rancher named Mason Garrett who wants our water. He took over Hostetter's range just east of here after Hostetter was killed. That was about two years ago."

"How did this Hostetter fella get killed?"

"He was shot in the back by rustlers. His wife found him out on their range. His body was riddled with bullets, and his herd was gone. She knew he had been fighting off rustlers, and when he didn't come home one night she rode out to look for him the next morning. Mrs. Hostetter went back east as soon as her husband was buried. People assume she sold the place to Garrett. He runs his cattle over there and some riders nobody knows are living in the bunkhouse."

John winced as Andrea poured whiskey over the hole in his shoulder. "Whew. It's a shame to waste good whiskey like that," he muttered.

"It will help keep down infection. You certainly don't need that on top of everything else. Here, hold tight to the end of this piece of cloth." Andrea ordered. She rebandaged the wound and began to clean the old bandages off the table. When she finished cleaning up John said, "I sincerely appreciate your help, but that was torture. I'll be lucky if I have enough strength left to eat."

"I'll help you. Let's get you back to bed and I can prop you up so you can rest while you eat."

"No. No. I'll stay here a little while longer. I'll be okay. Just give me a minute."

Andrea handed him a tin plate piled high with biscuits and meat and poured a cup of water for him to drink.

"This is good," John said between bites. "Will your folks miss these things?"

"I don't think so. I was careful about what I took. I brought you a shirt of Daddy's, but he doesn't wear it very often so I don't think it will be missed."

"Tell me about this rancher named Garrett. You said he wanted your water. Will your father sell out to him?"

"Oh no. I believe Daddy would die first. Sometimes I'm afraid it will come to that. Garrett has tried and tried to buy us out. He sent his foreman over just recently to offer Daddy a big price for the valley. He's got too many cattle for his range, even after pushing his largest herd onto Hostetter's place. Garrett really does need our water. Most of his original ranch is dry range except for a few springs. He has one dug well, but they're expensive. The last time Daddy refused to sell to him Garrett swore to Daddy that he meant to have Silver Creek someday and he didn't care how he got it."

"The same sort of things are happening to us that happened to Tim Hostetter. Two of our riders have been shot. One was killed. My brother Bill found him lying out on the range, two bullets in his back. Bill figured the man had been ambushed. He found a place in the brush nearby where someone had been standing. It appeared that he had waited there for a long time. He must have known the rider would be working in that area and lay in wait for him. Our cowboy obviously had no warning, and no chance, because he hadn't even touched his gun.

"We've lost a few cattle too. Even as protected as we are here. Daddy hired more riders to guard the herd, but it's hard to know who you're hiring."

"Do you suspect that Garrett is behind all this trouble?"

"It doesn't seem to fit his reputation, but no one else has any reason that we can figure to be harassing us. Garrett's range is on both sides of the opening to this valley. Silver Creek has more water on it than there is on all of Garrett's range, including a big pool on Hostetter's place. As far as we can tell, he's the only one who would benefit if we gave up and sold him the ranch."

Suddenly, Andrea realized she was doing all the talking. She felt a blaze of anger. "You know, Mr. Turner, you were supposed to be telling me your story, not trying to find out all about my family's business." She moved around to the other side of the table away from John.

John saw the change in Andrea's face. He realized her green eyes were full of anger and suspicion. "Here," he said, resting his weight on the back of his chair as he stood up. "Help me back over to the bunk and I'll tell you how I came to be lying where you found me."

With Andrea's shoulder supporting him under his good arm John was able to get back over to the bunk. He eased himself down and straightened out his legs. He was thinking fast. He couldn't tell the boy he was really Mason Garrett's son. Not yet, anyway. He was sure to assume he was up to no good. The next thing he would do would be to go home and tell Blaine and his riders that he was wounded and holed up in the cabin.

"I got in a gun fight over in Ellison Grove. I was just passing through town and went into the saloon for a drink. There was a half-drunk kid in the saloon that took exception to the way I drank my beer or something. He kept on jawing to his companion about what a fast draw he was. Finally he came over to where I was and started trying to prod me into drawing on him.

"I just sort of brushed him off and he left the saloon. When I finished my drink and went out to the street that kid was standing beside my horse. He had pulled my Henry off my saddle and held it over his head.

"I yelled for him to put it back where he found it and he laughed at me. He said that if I was too yellow to fight

I shouldn't carry a gun. I would still have ignored him if I could have, even after that, but the next instant he threw my rifle down in the street and drew on me. I shot him. I tried to shoot high. I think I caught him in his shoulder. I certainly didn't want to kill him.

"Of course everybody ran out of the saloon when they heard the shots. People were staring as though the boy was some sort of a show. I gathered up my rifle and stuck it back in the boot, getting ready to ride out of there. About that time the sheriff walked up. I recognized the man as an outlaw by name of Jake Thornton. A friend of mine once pointed him out to me in El Paso. He was known to be a real hard case. My friend said Thornton was not known to be much of a gunfighter, but he always rode with shady characters and was known to be dangerous.

"Thornton offered to put me in jail. He said the boy was his kin and if he died he would make sure that I'd be hung for his murder. I felt as though the crowd was closing in to help him, so I didn't even try to argue. I just knocked him down, jumped on Prince, and rode out of there as fast as I could.

"Thornton and some other fellows chased me for days. I came over the mountains and crossed a river at a deep canyon. I was across the water and up on the high side of the cut when Thornton and his men rode up on the other side. They were close enough that I could hear them cussing me, then Thornton and all the rest grabbed their rifles and began to shoot at me across the canyon.

"I spurred Prince up the trail, but one of the men dismounted to steady his shot and a bullet caught me in the shoulder before I could get into the rocks. I hung on to Prince's mane and rode well back into the rocks and stopped a minute to tie that shirt around me to try to stop the bleeding. I felt weak and I was dizzy from shock, but I stayed in the saddle somehow and headed for this cabin."

Candlelight flickered on her face as Andrea listened intently as John related the story. "How did you know this cabin was here?" she asked.

"A fella I rode with in Texas was from this country. His name was Jeb Deane. He described the valley to me and said he thought Alex Gunnison would like to have someone stop with him for a few months. Seems Jeb used to spend a lot of time hunting and fishing with Gunnison some years ago. I was headed here when I stumbled into that fracas in Ellison Grove. I won't be able to do much hunting in my condition, but I can sit and fish, I reckon."

"You'll be well soon," Andrea said. "I know Daddy won't mind you staying here until you get your strength back."

"Andy, please don't tell anyone I'm here, not for a little while," John asked. "Don't even tell your father. The more people who know I'm here the easier it will be for Thornton to find me if he follows me."

"But you said earlier that you had lost him." Andrea's face was hidden in the shadows. She didn't even try to keep the coldness of suspicion out of her voice. Suddenly, she felt sure this man wasn't telling a straight story.

"I think I did lose Thornton up there in the canyons, but you don't live long taking too many chances."

John heard the questioning in the boy's voice. He wondered how he could convince him to trust him. He needed time; at least enough time for his shoulder to heal to the point that he could get around again and defend himself if the need arose.

Andrea grabbed her hat. "I've got to go before my mother and father figure out that I'm not in my bed." She stared into John's face for a moment, then continued, "I promise I won't tell anyone you're here. At least not yet."

"Thanks, kid. You won't regret trusting me." John's voice was husky. A smile lifted one corner of his mouth.

Andrea dropped her head and ran out of the cabin.

"Funny kid," John said aloud. He stared at the closed door. Soon he slid down on the bunk and tried to find a more comfortable position. He went to sleep wondering what was so strange about the boy and if he really would keep quiet about helping a wounded stranger.

*   *   *

The track across the valley to the ranch buildings was easy to follow by moonlight. Andrea walked her pony around to the barn as quietly as she could and put him in his stall. She pulled his saddle off and tossed it over the side of the stall. Rubbing him down, she fed him an extra scoop of oats. When she climbed back into the window of her room the ranch was quiet.

Andrea went to bed wondering how long it would be before something else happened. *Will more men be killed?* she mused. *Is Billy going to be home tomorrow?* Andrea felt uneasy almost to the point of tears at the idea of deceiving her father. She had never lied to him, but if she kept Kyle Turner's presence at the cabin secret it would be necessary to lie. It was a sort of lie not to tell her father that the man was hiding in the cabin.

He's too weak and helpless to be any threat to us, she thought. *Except for that, I would tell. Still, it's too much of a coincidence for him to come here to this remote place just as the Garrett ranch is supposed to be hiring every gunman it can find. It could be that he's one of them.* Billy had heard talk in town weeks earlier that Mason Garrett was hiring any rider that would sign on and asking no questions. The story went that if the men were known to be better at shooting than at tending cows they were sure of a job at the Double G.

Rafe Willis was Garrett's foreman. He had grown up near Flagstaff and had a wild reputation. Someone in Hinton had told Russ Blaine that Willis had been in trouble over some stolen horses and left the country for a few years. Stories had drifted back that he was riding with outlaws in Kansas. He claimed to have killed men with his fists and bragged that he could out draw anyone with a handgun. Willis had come back to the area about two years earlier and signed on with Garrett. He was building a crew that was as rough and brutal looking a bunch of men as any outlaw band.

The first time any of the Blaine family had seen Rafe

A.H. Holt

Willis he rode into Silver Creek with Mason Garrett. That was the last time Garrett had come to the ranch. They came on a Sunday evening when Russ Blaine and his family were just finishing their dinner. Andrea wore a white dress and her hair loose on her shoulders. Julie Blaine always demanded that she dress like a lady on Sunday.

When she heard a knock on the back door, Andrea answered it expecting to see one of her father's riders. When she opened the door Rafe Willis and Garrett were standing on the porch. The look that came into Willis's eyes when he looked at her frightened Andrea and made her feel sick.

Willis was a tall and well-built man who looked to be about thirty-five. His eyes and hair were black and there was a nasty scar in front of his left ear. His face was Indian like and his skin was dark. He had high, broad cheekbones and a prominent nose. He stood on the porch and grinned down at Andrea with that awful expression until Garrett pushed past him and demanded to speak to her father.

Andrea called her father to the door, then hid in her room until the men left. It was significant that her father did not invite the men in and offer them a meal. It was almost sacrilege not to offer visitors a meal in such a remote area. She heard their footsteps as they moved off the porch to walk out toward the corral. Although she could hear the rumble of their voices, she couldn't make out what they were saying.

Andrea knew she would live in fear of meeting that man again. His wolflike expression made her feel weak and terrified. She would ride with her rifle in her hand from now on. Her heart pounded in disgust and anger every time she thought of the way he looked at her.

Chapter Three

Sleepily, Andrea snuggled under her quilt and thought about the wounded rider. Kyle Turner was tough looking, but it was a toughness of strength, not meanness. Even covered with several days' growth of dark beard and strained with pain, his face didn't frighten her. She thought he would be handsome when he was cleaned up.

I wonder how he will react when he realizes I'm a girl? she wondered. *Not like Rafe Willis did, I'm certain of that.*

As she slipped into sleep Andrea thought, *I'll never fool him when he's not groggy from loss of blood. He'll know I'm a girl the next time I go up to the cabin. I still don't think I'll be afraid of him, though.*

Early the next morning she woke to the sound of loud voices. She hurried to pull on her riding clothes and went into the kitchen. Her father was sitting at the kitchen table in a heated discussion with their foreman, Sandy Miller.

"Sandy, I want you to go up to the line shack and run Whitey and Burt off the ranch," Russ Blaine ordered.

Sandy had been their foreman since they started the ranch, and had always felt free to argue with Blaine if he didn't agree with him. "Now, Boss, don't let's go off half-cocked. Them boys have been working here for years now. Do you honestly think they would help Garrett do you any

39

harm? Do you seriously believe either one of those boys could be involved in Chuck Holden's killing?"

Blaine propped his elbows on the table and propped his chin on in his hands. He looked a little ashamed. "I don't rightly know what to think anymore, Sandy. Garrett's getting help from inside the valley, I'm as certain of that as I am that he wants to get his hands on my ranch so he'll have enough water to run all the cows he wants. But you have to remember, Andy saw those two boys meeting some rider up at Glade Spring yesterday. That just plain looks bad to me."

"I'll give you that," Sandy said, running one hand over his face. "I just can't believe them two boys would do you bad, boss. They've been our top hands. And I've known both of them boys since they were still wet behind their ears. Shucks, they were Chuck Holden's good friends. Besides, they hate that darn old range-hog Garrett just as much as you and me do."

"I thought they did, but if it wasn't Garrett's man they met, then who the heck could it have been, Sandy? You just tell me that." Russ Blaine's face showed the strain and worry of one of his men being murdered. That, added to long months of watching and waiting for something to happen was wearing on him. He believed the day would come that Mason Garrett would descend on his ranch with his vastly superior firepower. He couldn't admit it to his family or his riders, but he also believed that day would be the end of everything for him.

"It don't have to be anybody on the ranch helping Garrett, Boss. It would take fifty men to guard every spot where a single man or even three or four riders could get up over the rim and ride into the valley. He don't need the help of any of our riders to find out anything he wants."

"It's darn funny they can get in and run a bunch of cattle right out of the valley before anybody ever sees them." Blaine almost yelled in his disgust and frustration. The thought that some blasted thief could get a group of his cows out of the valley rankled on him. His losses had really been small. He had lost only a few cows, but it was as bad to him as if they had stolen hundreds.

"It shouldn't happen no more," said Sandy. "We've got the cattle down near the creek. It ain't going to be so easy for any more to get rustled. And Andy's out there watching. That gal don't miss much."

"Tell me what you think I should do about Whitey and Burt, Sandy?"

Sandy thought a moment before answering Blaine. He was a small man, slim and wiry. One of his shoulders was a little higher than the other one. It had been broken in a fall from a horse when he was only a boy. He had spent a lifetime riding and living outdoors. His face looked like it was carved from fine-grained mahogany. His reddish-brown hair and beard were streaked with white.

The foreman was plainly wrestling with his loyalties to Russ Blaine and those to his men. "Give Whitey and Burt the benefit of the doubt, please Boss? They've been good men."

"Sandy, I haven't paid the men in three months. I've been waiting till we drive some cattle to get the cash. I haven't been to the bank because I'm uneasy about borrowing money for expenses. Do you think those men would sell me out because they haven't been paid?"

"Doggone it, Boss, I know they wouldn't, and so do you." Sandy jumped out of his chair to pace up and down. "We've waited as long as six months for our money before, and we know you're good for it. That can't have a thing to do with two of our best men meeting some fella up near the rim."

"I'm going up ride out to Glade Spring today and brace them boys. If you'll just hang fire until I get back, I'll find out what's going on."

Russ Blaine looked up at Sandy's determined face. "Sure. You're right, Sandy. Whitey and Burt will have an explanation. Please don't tell them I had doubts of their loyalty. I'm feeling ashamed of myself already."

Thanks." Sandy chuckled as he grabbed his hat and started out the door. "I'll be back in a couple of hours."

When Sandy left the kitchen, Andrea brought two cups of coffee and sat down across the table from her father. "Daddy," she said, "I've been going up to Alec Gunnison's old cabin up above Silver Creek this week. I can see past the break in the rim from some rocks right up above the cabin. The spot I found gives me a clear view of most of the places where a rider could get in the valley. I can get home quickly from there too if I see anyone."

"That's fine, honey. Stay in the open, though. I worry about you roaming the woods. Your mother's right, you know. You're getting too grown up to be out alone like that so much. There're some rough men around here. Not all westerners show respect to a woman like they should, I'm afraid. If he gets up close, any man with eyes can tell you're a woman, even in that outfit."

Andrea looked ruefully at her worn jeans and heavy jacket; an old one of her brother's that was big enough to hide her shape. "I know, I know, Daddy." She grinned. "When all this mess with Garrett gets settled down I'll make me a fancy riding outfit with fringe on the sides and go around looking for a husband."

Blaine chuckled. He knew she was joking. Her mother was always complaining that Andrea was so much of a roughneck she would never find a husband. "Well girl," he said, patting her hand, "I'm in no hurry for you to find a husband and leave us. But your mother's right. Many western girls are married and have a couple of kids by the time they're your age."

"You talk like I'm ancient. I'd rather stay right here as long as I can." Andrea shook her curls and dropped her lashes to cover her eyes. Her father had accepted her wish to wear boy's clothes and learn to ride and shoot alongside her brother Bill when they first came west, but he had hinted several times lately that she had done it long enough. It was plain she would eventually have to stop running around free and accept the restrictions normally placed on a single woman.

As she finished her coffee, Andrea thought back to the frightening incident that had made her so painfully self-conscious about her femininity and so distrustful of men. When the Blaine family first came to Arizona they left their train at the crude station platform in Flagstaff. Andrea and her brother Bill somehow got separated from their mother and father in the crowd in front of the station house.

At only twelve years old Andrea was already showing the beauty she had inherited from her mother. Her dress and hat marked her as an easterner. Concerned at being separated from her parents, she tried to push her way through the muddle of people on the platform, clutching her handbag against her middle. As she reached the station house a rough hand grabbed her arm and she was jerked against a man's chest.

Andrea shuddered as she remembered the horrible, help-less feeling that enveloped her. She had screamed in terror. When she looked up into the man's eyes she had seen a look that she didn't fully understand but made her feel like an animal caught in a trap. She shuddered as she remem-bered that she had seen the same look in Rafe Willis' eyes when he stood on their porch that day.

The man at the station had laughed at her fear and held her against him, touching his drunken, whiskered face against hers. For the long moment it took for her father to push through the crowd to her side, she had almost fainted with fear and disgust. Russ Blaine knocked the man down and kicked him. He sent the station attendant to get the sheriff and had the man arrested for drunkenness and as-sault. Andrea sobbed for hours. For weeks afterward, she awakened almost every night, crying out in fear as she re-lived the nightmare.

Andrea didn't feel afraid of most men. She had just formed a habit of avoiding them as much as possible. She liked her father's riders and enjoyed joking and laughing with them. But they were steady, settled men who treated her with fond respect. Her mother lamented over her lost chances for parties and young men to court her since they were living in such an isolated location, but Andrea was content just as she was.

"I keep my pistol loaded and in my jacket pocket where it's easy to reach, Daddy, And you know I never go anywhere without my rifle. You don't have to worry about me.

"Say," she asked, hoping to get off the subject. "Is Billy home yet?"

"Not yet, honey. I know it's been more than a week. Like as not he had to wait over several days to see the sheriff or Judge Parker. The judge may have been out of town when he got there."

Blaine couldn't help looking worried. He knew Billy was a little wild. He had given him a special errand to tend to in town in addition to getting a wagonload of food supplies and extra ammunition for the ranch. He was afraid to guess what might be keeping the boy so long.

"Daddy, are you planning to make a drive soon?"

"We have to, honey. We're just about out of cash money. I haven't paid wages in close to three months. I'm feeling sort of skittish about going in debt for supplies. If I go to the bank for more money that skunk Asa Hamilton has already informed me I'd have to put the ranch up as collateral. If I do that Mason Garrett might be able to buy my note. I just can't take a chance on that, but my cash is almost gone so there is no way we can get out of making a drive."

"Do you think Garrett will try to interfere with the roundup or the drive?"

"I don't know. Heck, the way things are going we may have to shoot our way out of the valley." Blaine shook his head as though in despair.

"I've been waiting and hoping Garrett would get involved in his own roundup, so we could drive a few head without any trouble. It looks like he's not going to sell anything at all this year. Or it's possible he's hired so many riders he can keep some after us and still have enough men left to make a roundup."

"How long can we hold out if we can't sell any cattle?" Julie Blaine asked from the hall doorway. She had been listening to their conversation.

Blaine was obviously shaken. He had hoped to keep the worst of his problems away from his wife. "I've hated to worry you, Julie, but we won't hold out much longer without money for wages and supplies. Our riders will start leaving us eventually if they're not paid, and no one can blame them if they do."

Angela shook her head. "No, Daddy, you're wrong. They'll not leave us. They've been with us too long and they're too loyal to leave us in such a bad place just because of money."

"I hope you're right, honey, and that may be, but finding Chuck Holden murdered isn't going to help. We can keep the cattle safe in this valley but a sharpshooter can sit up on the rim and pick the men off one by one. That's enough to spook anybody, I don't care how loyal they are."

"I think it's made the men mad more than anything. I talked to Will and Randy yesterday morning when I was saddling my pony. They were ready to go find Mason Garrett and Rafe Willis and shoot them down."

"I just can't believe Garrett would send killers out to ambush my men." Blaine shook his head. "Maybe he'd ride in here with an army and kill us all, but I think if he did, he would do it openly."

"It would hardly help anyone other than Mason Garrett to kill our men," Julie Blaine argued.

"I can't figure it out. Sandy looked the ground over up there and found where two men had hidden in the rocks for hours waiting for Holden to come along the track. It just won't figure." Blaine reached over and patted his wife's hand. "Don't you go worrying about it, honey. Billy's reporting Chuck's shooting to the sheriff, maybe he can find something."

Andrea asked, "Did Sandy try to follow the tracks?"

"Yes, he went up over the rim and as far as that big grove of pines before he lost their trail. It sure looked like they were headed for the Double G. It's less than a mile to Garrett's corrals and bunkhouse from the other side of that bunch of pines. Sandy couldn't see which way the trail went after the men entered the woods. The ground's covered in pine needles so thick you can't see tracks."

"Will the sheriff believe that?" Andrea asked. "I mean, will he believe the men came from Garrett's place?"

"I don't think we can count on getting much help from O'Reilly. He's bright enough to see that Garrett's bucking to be top man around here, but I don't think he'll be willing do any thing against him."

"Russ, you don't really think the sheriff would help Garrett against us?" Julie Blaine looked horrified and more worried than ever.

Andrea could see the anger in her father's eyes as he talked. He looked ready to do something violent. The strain of constantly being on guard against Garrett or whoever it was that had been harassing them was showing. The experience of having one of his men bushwhacked and killed almost on his doorstep was unnerving. Blaine was more than unsettled and bewildered, he was almost desperate.

Andrea got up from the table and started toward the pantry. She announced, "I'm going to take a coffeepot and some bacon to cook for my dinner today, Daddy. So if anyone sees smoke up top it'll just be me. I'll use the fireplace in Gunnison's old cabin. I thought I would starve a couple of days this week, and I wished for a cup of coffee to warm me up several times." Taking an old coffeepot and a tin frying pan from the shelf, Andrea slipped some more bacon, some coffee, and other supplies in a sack. She leaned over to kiss her mother's cheek then ran out the back door.

Russ Blaine didn't seem to notice anything, but Julie got up to stand at the back door with her hands on her hips watching Andrea as she ran to the barn. She turned back to her husband and said, "Russ, that girl is up to something."

"What do you mean, up to something?"

"She took enough food for four or five meals. What could she be doing? Do you think she could be meeting someone up on the hills?"

"Now, Julie, stop your worrying about Andrea. That girl's as good as gold and you know it."

"I don't mean that, Russ. I'm just worried about her." Julie wrung her hands and left the room. She knew it was hopeless to say anything. Russ would never hear any criticism of Andrea's actions.

The black pony was waiting for Andrea and nickered a greeting as she entered his stall. She rubbed his soft nose as he ate the apple she took from her coat pocket, and then she threw her saddle on his back and tied the girth. She secured the pack to the straps behind her saddle and mounted. Just outside the barn she urged Pat to a run, rounding the side of the house and leaving the yard by the main gate.

The open meadows were lush and green. This creek-watered grass was what made Silver Creek Ranch so attractive to a cattleman. Andrea could see the herd in the distance. Their dark backs glinted in the sun. The men had pushed them closer to the ranch buildings to keep them safe.

The man she knew as Kyle Turner was sitting on the cabin doorstep when Andrea rode into the clearing. As she dismounted she noticed that he had on the clean shirt she brought for him and his hair was combed smooth. She felt her heart skip a beat when she saw how handsome he was, even with the dark beard on his cheeks. His face was a little pale but he looked much better.

"Good morning," she called, "I see you're feeling better."

"You bet," John answered, grinning broadly. "I hope you

brought some more of those biscuits, I think I'm dying of starvation."

Andrea kept her hat pulled down over her face as she untied the pack from her saddle. She held the bulky pack in front of her as she walked over to stand near John. "I told my father I was coming up here to watch for intruders in the valley, and that I would make a fire to cook my dinner. I'll be able to cook you a hot meal today, but first I have to tell you something."

John's face stiffened and he looked up at her with wary eyes. Had she betrayed him?

"It has nothing to do with you," Andrea said hastily. "I said I wouldn't tell anyone you were here and I keep my word. If I change my mind and feel I have to tell someone, I'll tell you first."

Relaxing, John leaned back against the doorjamb. "Thanks, kid. What did you want to tell me?"

Andrea hung her head for a moment then lifted it high, and looked straight into John's eyes. "I'm not a boy."

John's eyes widened and he pulled himself up to his feet. He started to speak then stopped to stare at her with his mouth open. He was completely surprised for an instant, but then he remembered noticing her smooth white arms and slim hands. He had gone to sleep puzzling over what was strange about the kid. Disgusted with himself for being so thickheaded and thoroughly annoyed with the girl for fooling him, he glared at her. His face clouded and he barked out angrily, "That's a lowdown trick to pull on a man."

Andrea watched as his face turn red and tried not to smile. She answered him softly. "I didn't tell you I was a boy, Mr. Turner. You just assumed I was a boy from my clothes and my nickname."

"Andy's no name for a girl." Anger mingled with embarrassment made John's voice harsh.

"Please don't feel embarrassed, Mr. Turner. You haven't done anything to be embarrassed about. I wear these clothes and tell people my name is Andy because I couldn't ride around the country like I do if everybody knew I was a girl. I wouldn't be free to be myself."

"You mean you pull that stunt on other people too?" John said sarcastically. He leaned his good shoulder against the doorway and stared down at her with one eyebrow raised.

It was Andrea's turn to be embarrassed. "It's not easy to be a girl here. There are men that I'd be afraid of if they knew I was a girl." Her voice pleaded for him to understand.

"So you run around the country in boy's pants. That right there might give some men the wrong idea about a girl, you know."

Andrea felt her temper rising. "What I do is just none of your business, Mr. Turner. Do you want me to fix you some food or not?"

John looked at her steadily for a moment, then hung his head. He was calming down. "Forgive me, Miss Blaine. I'd appreciate the food. I appreciate all you have done for me." Turning, he entered the cabin and took a seat at the table.

Andrea quickly built a fire and started water heating for coffee. She could feel the man's eyes on her as she worked. She sliced bacon with an unsteady hand and settled the full frying pan on the fire.

"I brought a loaf of white bread that my mother baked this morning. It should still be warm. I'll bet she makes the best bread you ever tasted. Anyone who has ever eaten at our table brags about how good it is. I'll cook some extra bacon so you'll have something to eat later."

"That'll be good. I've got beans and flour and a little chunk of bacon in my pack. I could make out fine if I could have a fire. I'm going to try to get out of here tomorrow or the next day."

Andrea started up from the hearth. "You don't have to do that, Mr. Turner. Stay as long as you need to. If you try to ride too quickly that wound might open and start bleeding again. Besides, you're too weak to leave yet."

John shrugged and shook his head. "It doesn't look right

for you to keep coming here, Miss Blaine. Your father would shoot me down for letting you do it and he'd have good reason."

Andrea's eyes met his and held. "I'm not afraid of you, Mr. Turner. I wasn't even afraid when you were angry. I would explain what happened to my father if he found out, and he would understand."

"Afraid of me." John repeated wiping his face with his hand. He was obviously shaken. "I should hope you wouldn't be scared of me. I'm not in the habit of molesting young girls and besides, I'm so weak you could knock me down with one hand if you wanted to."

Laughing, Andrea placed his food on the table. She filled a plate for herself and sat down across from him. John hung his head and refused to look at her. They ate the bacon and bread without speaking. Andrea pulled the coffeepot off the fire when it boiled and poured them both a cup.

John watched the girl's deft movements. She had removed her hat while she was working and her brown hair was a riot of tangled curls down on her shoulders. The fire reddened her cheeks. The glow of the flames emphasized the beauty of her well-shaped face and straight little nose. Long, dark eyelashes brushed against her cheeks as she worked close to the fire. His heart lurched when she laughed.

She's so beautiful, he thought. *I wonder what she'd look like in a dress?* Amazed, he wondered how he could ever have thought this girl was a boy no matter how she dressed. He must have been delirious from the loss of blood.

"Please stop staring at me, Mr. Turner." The girl's voice surprised him. She was sipping her coffee and watching him over the rim of her tin cup.

"Oh, I beg your pardon, Miss Blaine. I guess I'm still a little shocked."

"I'm sorry. Please forgive me for fooling you. Will you try to understand my side of it?" Andrea lowered her cup as she spoke. Her face was white and serious. Her mouth quivered slightly.

"Don't think of it again, please. I had no right to yell at you. I was just completely surprised," John said, obviously stricken by her distress.

"My real name is Andrea, if you can't call me Andy any longer won't you please call me that?"

Her voice was soft and definitely feminine. *No wonder she has to hide from men,* John thought. "I'd be honored to call you Andrea. I hope you'll call me Kyle," John said, feeling lower than low for lying to her.

Andrea laughed. "Thank you, Kyle."

"Oh," she continued as she turned her head to the side and gave him a questioning look. "I thought I heard a little hesitation when you told me your name yesterday. Is it possible that maybe you were hiding a little something from me as well?"

"I guess you're right to suspect that I didn't tell you everything, but my name is Kyle." John was able to look her in the eye as he spoke because he had used his middle name and his mother's maiden name. It wasn't a complete lie.

"Miss Blaine, I promise you that the things I'm not telling you can bring no harm to you or your people. Please believe that. I'm truly grateful for all you've done for me. I know you saved my life by helping me."

"I don't expect your gratitude for what I did. Anyone would have helped you. If you have secrets, that's all right with me. Something tells me I can trust you. I'll keep riding up here every day until you can ride. I often use this place as my lookout post. I'll remind my folks and our riders that I'll be lighting a fire occasionally to make me some coffee and warm my food. That way no one will suspect anyone else is here."

Andrea stood up then and collected the plates and utensils. "I have to get up on the rocks and see if I can see anything. I'll clean these up later. You'd better get some rest."

"What are you watching for?" John asked.

"Sometimes I'm not completely sure. Riders have been

coming into the valley to shoot at our men and steal our cattle. I'm hoping that if they do it again I will see them in time to warn our riders. One of our men was shot from ambush and killed several days ago over at the other end of the valley. We couldn't find the men who did it, and we are not sure the county sheriff will even look for them.

"Our riders are holding our main herd at the other end of the valley where they can protect them from rustlers. That part of the valley is too far from here for me to iden- tify riders, even with my glass, but I can recognize our horses. If I see a strange rider I'm supposed to signal to the men who are watching the herd."

John sat at the table thinking long after the girl left the cabin. He puzzled over the things she said, trying to fit them into the story Alec Gunnison told him about the sit- uation at Silver Creek.

Chapter Four

Andrea led her pony through the woods to the little meadow where Prince was hobbled. The big horse stopped grazing to nicker a hello when she came out of the trees. She unsaddled her pony and turned him loose to roll and graze. He would stay in the vicinity of the meadow until she came for him. Taking her telescope and rifle she followed a faint trail around the spring to climb up toward the large, flat rock she used as a lookout post.

The large pines around the cabin soon gave way to smaller growth among clusters of rocks as Andrea followed the trail higher. She had to use her hands to pull herself up the steeply sloping path. When she finally gained the highest point she stooped low to keep her head below the top of the stunted trees and brush that extended above the rock in case someone happened to be looking at that exact spot.

Climbing out on the flat boulder, she lay down near the edge and looked down over the valley. She could see for miles. She slowly scanned the walls of the rim on the far side, beyond the herd that was peacefully grazing on the long grass. Her telescope brought the distant wall of hills close enough to see any horse or man that moved. She stopped the glass and slowly scrutinized any place in the rim that looked low enough for a rider to come down into the valley. When she could see nothing high up, she studied the lower slopes just as carefully, stopping the glass on every outcropping of rock and any space not covered in trees.

Satisfied at last that no one was in the valley that didn't belong there she closed the glass and sat up to gaze out over the valley floor. The herd was over on the western side of the creek near the ranch buildings. From her position, the road from the ranch to the opening in the valley wall looked like a reddish brown rope snaking through the green grass. It went out of sight as it curved around a hill and joined the trail that ran up to the top of the rim and out onto the open range.

It was late afternoon when Andrea first noticed a plume of dust rising beyond the hills to the south. She trained her glass on the road. Soon a large wagon appeared. It had four riders beside it. Andrea had never seen any of their horses before. She recognized the rig and her brother's horse tied to the tailgate of the wagon.

"Billy," she said aloud. "It's about time." She had been worried sick about her brother. He had been sent to town for supplies and to get the sheriff more than a week ago. She had expected him to come home almost a week before this.

The wagon was obviously carrying a heavy load. She watched as the driver stopped at the crest of the hill. She recognized her brother's shape as he jumped to the ground from the high seat. He motioned to the men riding with him to help him. Two of them got down from their horses. Working together, they began to roll a heavy log from the roadside. They worked the log into the middle of the road behind the wagon and chained it to both sides of the rear axle.

The steep, downward slope of the entrance road always required a drag for a wagon with a heavy load to make it down safely. Without the big log holding back on the weight of the wagon it would push against the horses and force them to run to stay out of its way. It took time to make two stops to attach a drag and remove it every trip, but it prevented accidents.

Andrea used her glass to examine the strangers riding with Billy but she couldn't recognize either of them or their horses. Sheriff O'Riley definitely wasn't among them. He was a tall, heavy man and always rode a big, rawboned, black horse. These men were lean and rode like cowboys. Their horses were mustangs. Finally giving up on trying to identify the men, Andrea rationalized that maybe Billy had convinced the men to ride for them.

She watched until the wagon reached the bottom of the slope and stopped to release the drag. It would still take an hour or more for them to reach the ranch buildings. Training her glass to the far side of the hills again Andrea resumed her careful search of the area. When she was satisfied that no one else had come into the valley, she climbed down from the boulder and slid over the ridge to make her way back down to the meadow.

Entering the clearing, Andrea whistled for her pony. He came trotting to her, begging for a treat. "I don't have anything for you, Pat." She rubbed his nose. "Wait until we get home and I'll get you another apple."

She stroked the horse's nose and ears for a few minutes then saddled quickly and led him down the path to the front of the cabin. She dropped his reins on the ground so he would stand as she went in the open door.

John was sitting by the fire. "I wondered if you were going to stay up there all night. I made a fresh pot of coffee."

"Coffee sounds great," she said. "I'll start some bacon frying then have a cup with you before I go." Andrea placed her glass on the table and pulled off her gloves.

After she started the bacon cooking, she took the water bucket and re-filled it. She made several trips outside for firewood, stacking it against the inside wall at the front of the cabin, away from the fireplace. She decided to take the time to split some heart pine kindling for starting the fire quickly if necessary. Finding no axe near the woodpile, she went over to her saddle and removed the small hatchet she always carried. She often used it to build a small fire when she was hunting. Splitting a pine knot into a small quantity of kindling, she went back to the cabin.

"I'm sorry you can't keep the fire going all night," she said as she brought the bundle of lightwood splinters into the cabin and placed it on top of the stack of wood. "It always gets cool enough for a fire to feel good up here in the late evening at this time of year."

"The cabin's warm now, and that'll last until I go to sleep," John said. "Sleep seems to be all I want to do, anyway."

"I reckon you're sleepy because you're weak from losing so much blood. That'll pass in a day or two if you take it easy and eat as much as you can. How does your shoulder feel today?"

"It hardly hurts unless I move too much. I'll be okay in a few more days. A wound like this isn't so bad if you don't get fever with it. I'm just thankful the bullet went all the way through."

"Have you been wounded before?" Andrea studied the man's face as she prepared his meal. He was turned away from her slightly, looking into the fire. He had shaved off his dark beard and appeared much younger. The skin on his face and hands was bronzed from living outdoors. His heavy black hair fell down into his eyes and gave him a foreign look.

For a second it seemed as though there was something slightly familiar about the set of his head and his wide shoulders. *Now why did I think that?* she thought, as she cut bacon and dropped it into the hot frying pan.

"Did you see anything going on in the valley today?" John asked, turning toward her in his chair.

"No, I saw no one. That is, I saw no one except my brother and some riders that were with him. He's finally come back from town. He went in for supplies and to report the death of one of our riders. He was due back home days ago. I was worrying about him. He's sometimes a little reckless and seems to attract trouble. I'm anxious to get home to see why he was so late and if he found out anything to help us."

When the meal was ready Andrea refused to eat. "I have to get on home. I think I'll pass on more coffee. I want to find out who those men were who were riding with Billy."

John saw the worry in her face. Anxiously, he stopped eating to ask, "Will you come back tomorrow?"

"I'll be here," Andrea said. Without looking at John again she picked up her telescope and gloves from the table and stepped outside to mount her pony.

Andrea walked her pony down the path until the woods opened up, then she urged him to a canter. Months of tension and worry over the constant threats to her father's riders and fear over what Garrett might do next were heavy on her mind. Something had to happen soon.

Bill Blaine drove the heavily loaded wagon up close to the back porch of the ranch house. He left it positioned so the supplies intended for the family could be easily unloaded into the kitchen storeroom. He and one of the men with him unhooked the draft horses from the wagon and led them to the barn. Bill pulled the harness from the backs of the horses and gave them each grain while the man helping him rubbed the tired horses down. The other riders unsaddled the riding horses, and wiped their backs with their saddle blankets. At Bill Blaine's direction the men fed their horses some grain then turned them loose in the corral, placing their saddles and bridles on the rack in the aisle between the stalls.

The four strange cowboys walked across the yard to the house with Bill. Russ Blaine met them on the back porch. Bill was bubbling over with excitement as he called out to his father. "Come and meet Uncle Malcolm Ames's son, Dad."

Blaine started visibly as he examined the face of the foremost man. "Malcolm Ames's son," he exclaimed.

"Well, come up here where I can see you, son. Your name's Nelson isn't it?"

The solid young cowboy reached for Blaine's outstretched hand. "I'm Nelson, Mr. Blaine. Thanks for remembering me. When Dad got your letter asking him to send you some riders you could trust he thought you'd feel better to have somebody you knew you could count on."

"You look just like your father, son. It'll give me strength just to see you here." Blaine clung to the cowboy's hand. "Darn if looking at you isn't like going back twenty years. You've got the same red hair and devilish grin that got your father into every scrape a young man could find back home in Moultrie."

Nelson Ames laughed aloud. His square, freckled face looked like that of a boy half his age. "Dad claims you were the one that got into all the scrapes, Mr. Blaine. He swears he only got in trouble when he was helping you out of a fix."

"I can see I'll have to straighten you out before you go back home. I'll bet I can tell you some stories your daddy hasn't had the nerve to tell you yet."

Nelson turned to his companions. "Let me introduce the three fellows with me, Mr. Blaine. The Comanche looking fella here is Tip Blackwell and these two scrawny boys hiding behind him are Juan and Ernesto Bates. We've been friends for years. Tip has been riding for Dad ever since we came to Arizona, and the Bates family owns the ranch next to ours. You can count on them Sir, just like you can count on me."

Ernesto Bates spoke up. "I'm pleased to finally meet you, Mr. Blaine. We've heard Mr. Ames spin yarns about you and him for years."

"Howdy boys," Blaine said as he shook the hand first of Ernesto then Juan. "There is no way I can tell you how much I appreciate your coming here. You just might save my hide, and you will surely save my ranch. Let's head for the bunkhouse. We'll get you settled in, then Nelson and

Billy and I can talk. We might even decide on something we can do."

Russ Blaine suddenly felt so pleased he laughed out loud. These young men didn't seem to be the least afraid or concerned about any trouble they might be walking into. He had appealed for help from his oldest friend and his answer had been to send these four strong young men. He knew he could put complete faith in them. It was as if each one of them was his old friend Malcolm Ames himself come to stand beside him because he was in trouble.

Tip Blackwell didn't extend his hand, but stepped closer to Blaine. He was not young but he was still strong and straight. He was much taller than the other men and his bulky shoulders were covered in a buckskin shirt decorated with colored designs. He wore black pants that were tight around his powerful legs. He wore no handgun, but carried a rifle in his right hand. His face was brown and smooth and his eyes shone a glittering black.

"I am proud to meet Ames's friend," he said. His voice was deep and harsh and his words were slightly accented.

"I'm thankful to have you here, Blackwell. You must be the friend that Malcolm refers to as Red Lance." Blaine's tone expressed his curiosity about the man, but he didn't ask questions. His friend had mentioned how much he depended on Blackwell in several letters.

The Indian chuckled softly and nodded as he answered, "Yes, I have been called Red Lance." He stepped back behind the other riders without offering any further explanation.

Blaine turned to the group. "You boys will find everything you need at the bunkhouse. Billy will introduce you to Sandy Miller. He's our foreman and you'll like him. He's been with us since we first got the ranch. We'll get together tomorrow and map out a plan. Nelson, we'll fix you up in our guest room."

"Don't bother about that, Mr. Blaine," Nelson said. "I'd actually rather stay in the bunkhouse with these boys."

"If that's what you'd rather do, that's fine, but you're

welcome to stay in our home, Nelson, we'd be honored to
have you."

"I appreciate that sir, but I'm going to stay right here in
the bunkhouse. I think I'll most likely find out more about
your problems if I'm just another one of your riders."

"You're probably right, at that," Blaine said, "but come
up to the house with us now and talk. I want to hear about
how your father is doing and my wife will want to know
about your mother and the rest of your family."

After they had met Sandy Miller and settled the men in
the bunkhouse, Nelson Ames joined Russ and Billy around
the kitchen table. Julie Blaine excitedly welcomed the son
of their old friends and asked after his mother and his two
sisters. When the greetings were over, she turned to the
stove and poured a cup of coffee for each man, then she
entered the pantry and bringing out an apple pie, she placed
a generous slice in front of each of them.

The big freight wagon was backed up to the back porch
when Andrea rode into the yard. She noticed that the four
strange horses she had seen earlier were standing in the
corral. As she led her pony into his stall she patted the
noses of the draft horses, glad to see them back in their
stalls where they belonged. When she finished feeding and
grooming her pony she hurried out of the barn and up
to the house. As she washed her hands and face on the
porch she could hear men talking in the kitchen. Hearing
a voice she didn't know she didn't want to go into the
kitchen, so she entered the house by her window and
stepped quietly across the room to listen at the door.

As they were enjoying their pie and coffee, Nelson Ames
said, "Dad let me read your letter, Mr. Blaine. I had a lot
of questions and gaps in my understanding of your situation, but Bill has filled me in most of them on the way here
out from town." His eyes were serious.

"It seems to me that there's someone else besides Garrett
involved in the trouble you're having. I asked around about
Garrett when we were in Hinton. He's known as a hard

man that will take what he can get, but not for back shooting and cattle rustling. Actually, after reading your letter to Dad, I was surprised by it, but the people I talked with in town seem to sort of look up to the man."

"You know something son," Blaine said, nodding his agreement. "That thought's been haunting me for months. The shooting of Chuck Holden and the raids on my cattle don't fit with what I know about Mason Garrett at all. He's a determined old devil, and won't hesitate to push to get his way, but I just can't believe he'd be responsible for two killings. It just doesn't fit."

Nelson continued talking, "While I was waiting for Bill to get the supplies loaded, I did some talking and listening around the mercantile and I also talked some with the bartender in the saloon. I understand that Garret's foreman is a known gunman with a bad reputation."

"Rafe Willis is a bad one. Garrett took him on as foreman about two years ago. Garrett's only son, Johnny, I think his name was, left home about that time. The son was his foreman up until about the time we bought this place. There was some sort of big row over there and Garrett threw his boy off the place. People said it was the old story of a father not wanting to let his son grow up. The boy was said to be a little wild and he was handy with a gun I hear, but mostly he was well liked."

"The story is that Garrett tried to whip his boy over something and the boy decided he'd had enough." Blaine continued, "I certainly don't blame him, I understand the old man tried to use a bullwhip on him and the boy took the whip away from his father and knocked him down. He told Mason Garrett that if he ever hit him with the whip he'd use his gun on him. Nobody's heard of the boy since."

"I've also been told that after young Garrett left, his father went through three or four other foremen before he hired Willis. Now Willis seems to be running the ranch on his own. I heard that lately he even does all of Garrett's money business, buying, selling, and paying the hands. He came here to the house without Garrett a few weeks ago.

He had two ugly rannys with him that I had never seen before, and they almost pushed their way in the house.

"Willis stood out there on the porch and made me a big offer for this place in Garrett's name. When I refused to sell he cursed me for a fool and said I'd be glad to sell when he was done with me. I blew up then and told him to get off my land or I'd shoot him where he stood. I had just happened to answer the door with my rifle in my hand. It was after that when we started to have real trouble around here, what with losing cattle and having our riders shot from ambush."

Bill spoke up, "Dad, do you think Willis is doing things on his own without Garrett knowing about them?"

"That has to be the answer, son, and it makes me feel better to say it. I've been so mad for a while I haven't been thinking clearly."

"Well it doesn't exactly make me feel any better," said Nelson. "I can shoot, but I'm no match for a gunman. Men like that can't be beat except with a gun. Can any of your outfit handle Willis or any of his gun fighters in a stand-up gunfight?"

"Heck no," Blaine said. "My men are just good at working cows. Most of them are getting along in years like myself. We'd do all right in a fight, or defending the ranch from a raid. They've got plenty of nerve. It's not that. Give them a chance and my riders would charge Hades with a bucket of water. But none of us could face up to a fast gun. Billy here likes to think he's fast, but he's nowhere near fast enough to stand up to an experienced gunman."

"I might be fast enough, Dad," said Bill, a hopeful look on his face.

Nelson looked at Bill a moment and said in a disgusted voice, "You might just be dead too, my friend. How would your Mother and Dad feel then?"

"Aw, Nels, you make me feel awful." Bill lowered his red face in embarrassment.

"I'm sorry, Billy. I don't want you to get shot."

Nelson tried to change the subject. "Say Bill, where's that pretty little sister of yours?"

"Yeah, Dad." Bill turned to his father. "Is Andy still riding up on the rim every day to watch the valley?"

"She sure is. And I couldn't be prouder of the job she's doing. She should be home in a few minutes. I'm sure she spotted the wagon as you were coming in. She doesn't miss much. She's been grumbling about you not coming home for the last two or three days now."

"Oh, Mr. Blaine," asked Nelson. "Billy thought that judging from past performance, he didn't think we could count on any help from the Hinton sheriff if it came to a shooting war, do you think the same thing?"

"Shucks, Nelson, that drunken bog jumper is in Garrett's or Willis's pocket, one or the other, I'm not real sure which. He always has been in somebody's pocket. He follows the man he thinks will be the winner in any dispute, or the one who will pay him the most money. He'll fiddle around and then take everything he learns straight to one of them for instructions on how to do his job. The story I get is that Willis and a couple of town men make sure O'Riley gets a little extra in his pay envelope every month. I have no intention of paying him to help me and he knows it."

"Mr. Blaine, it seems to me you think Garrett's basically a decent man, and if you agree," Nelson Ames said thoughtfully, "that may help you."

"I don't know about it helping me any. Garrett is a stubborn and prideful old man. If Willis got out of hand and went against him, I don't know if he'd ever admit it. He might just cover it up as long as he could. I can't see him owning up to needing help, no matter what happened."

Nelson stood up and turned to face Bill Blaine. "I'll say good night now, Bill, and to you too, Mr. Blaine. It's great being here, but this has been a long day. I'm just not used to such long rides. The boys and me will try to get to know your crew and then get ourselves bedded down. We'll worry about this thing tomorrow."

"You're right, Nelson," Russ Blaine said. "All I can see

to do now is to protect my cattle and men as best I can until something else happens. Maybe a good night's rest will help us all think of something different."

Blaine stepped out on the porch and watched as Nelson Ames walked across the back yard toward the bunkhouse. Blaine's expression was quiet, almost happy. His eyes glowed with hope that these new men would help him settle this trouble.

When Andrea heard the man leave, she gave him enough time to get well away from the house then she stepped out of her room and through the kitchen to the porch. She slipped her arm through her father's. "I heard everything, Daddy. Isn't Nelson Ames a fine-looking boy?"

Blaine looked down at her smiling face. "You might not have to dress up and go looking for a husband after all, baby girl. You couldn't do better than to marry Malcolm Ames's boy."

"Oh for heaven sakes, Daddy," Andrea scolded. She could feel her face flaming. "The poor man probably has a sweetheart at home. Don't you dare say anything like that to him."

"Well calm down, for goodness sakes." Blaine was astonished at her reaction. "I was just thinking out loud."

"I'd appreciate it if you would just keep such thoughts to yourself. I'd like to do my own husband choosing if you don't mind." Andy withdrew her hand from her father's arm and rushed into the house, slamming the door.

"Can you beat that," Blaine muttered to himself. "I'll invite that boy to eat supper with us every night. Think of it. Mine and Julie's girl and Malcolm's boy together, that would be just about perfect. Wouldn't Julie love that?" Still smiling, he filled his pipe and sat down on the porch step to savor the idea. He didn't think of the ranch or range troubles for the first time in weeks.

Chapter Five

The sheriff rode into Silver Creek three days later. Sean O'Riley was running to fat as he got older. He had been a Sargent in the army during the Apache Indian troubles, stationed down at Fort Bayard. The only visible evidence left of his time in the military was his bearing when he was in the saddle. He had left the army after the Indian troubles were settled and moved into a rooming house in Hinton. He did nothing but hang around the saloon and play cards until he was appointed sheriff by the town council. He was supposed to be responsible for law enforcement in the whole county, but he did just enough to keep the town of Hinton quiet, hardly noticing any problems that happened outside the town's limits unless he was pushed into it. O'Riley still spent much more of his time in the town's only saloon than he did in his office. His red face and excess weight marked him as a hard drinker.

One deputy rode with O'Riley. Del Ketchum had been a rider for the Hostetter spread before the rancher was killed. Garrett or his foreman had evidently fired Hostetter's whole outfit when he took over the property. All of the riders but Ketchum had drifted away to find other work. Ketchum had hung around town for a few months, doing odd jobs to earn his living, and O'Riley finally hired him

65

as his deputy. He quickly acquired the reputation of liking his liquor as much as the sheriff did.

Julie Blaine noticed the Sheriff and his deputy approaching the house and thought that the two men were arriving unusually early. She puzzled over that for a few minutes then assumed that they must have camped out all night, or perhaps spent the night at the Garrett ranch, because the sun was just coloring the sky over the rim as they rode into the ranch yard. It took several hours to ride to Silver Creek from Hinton.

The two men dismounted and tied their horses to a front porch post. O'Riley's horse looked huge. He certainly had to be big and strong to carry the man's weight all day. It was a rough-coated brute of a horse that appeared to suit the Irishman's reputation. Ketchum's horse was a small gray mustang. He patted the mustang's nose and spoke softly to him as he dismounted. He dropped his reins to the ground and his horse stood still, ground-hitched.

Ketchum was as slim and wiry as O'Riley was big. His hair was a nondescript brown and his pale blue eyes looked almost white in his leathery face. He was not given to speech and seemed to fade into the background as Julie Blaine invited he and O'Riley into the house.

"Both of you come on through to the kitchen, Sheriff," Julie Blaine said as she led the way through the house. "Russ is out at the bunkhouse. I'll pour you some coffee and ring the bell for him then I'll fix you men some food."

"Don't you go to no bother now, Miz Blaine," O'Riley said. "I shore do love your light bread, though. It's been a regular age since I tasted it." Both men removed their hats and followed her through the main room and into the kitchen.

Smiling, Julie Blaine said, "Sit down, then. I'll have some food ready for you before Russ gets here."

After she went to the back porch and rang the big iron bell twice, Julie pulled the coffeepot to the front of the iron cook stove. Adding several small sticks of fat pine to make a hot fire, she quickly cut enough slices of bacon to fill a frying pan and set it directly on the flame. As soon as the bacon had started browning, she broke several eggs into another frying pan.

In keeping with the practice in the country, visitors who came to the ranch near mealtime were always invited to the table. Julie Blaine enjoyed the custom. She was an expert cook and relished the praise her cooking always received. She soon placed plates piled with crisp bacon, fried eggs, and thick slices of homemade bread in front of the two men. They were almost finished eating when Russ Blaine stepped into the kitchen.

"Good morning, Sheriff. Good morning, Del," he said as he hung his hat on a peg near the door. "I appreciate you riding all the way out here."

"It's my job, Mr. Blaine," answered the sheriff brusquely. "I ain't found out a thing except that your son said your man was shot with what appeared to be a .44 caliber bullet. Of course, that means the shooter could be just about anybody in this territory." O'Riley looked ill at ease and spoke a little too loudly.

"What are you planning to do about it?" Blaine asked. His voice had an accusing note in it. "You know this is the second time one of my men has been shot from ambush. The first time it happened the bullet just creased the man's arm, but this time it's cold-blooded murder, plain and simple."

"Mr. Blaine, I rode up here to find out anything I can," O'Riley said defensively. "If you'll send one of your men with me to show me exactly where the shooting happened, I'll try to back-track the killer."

"Forget that, any trail he left is long gone by this time. Sandy Miller and I already tracked him over the rim to that grove of tall pines near Garrett's place. We lost his trail up there in the thick pine needles. We circled around and searched, but we never could find the place where he rode out of the woods. Garrett's got cattle grazing all around on the other side of those pines and the man must have hidden his tracks by riding through the herd."

O'Riley looked more uncomfortable and shifted in his chair before he spoke. "Are you trying to say something, Blaine?"

Blaine leaned against the table and looked down at the sheriff. "I got out what I was trying to say, O'Riley." His voice was icy. "What were you trying to say?"

"Darn it man, you can't think that bushwhacker came from Garrett's ranch, or that he had anything to do with it."

"I don't know why I can't," Blaine was almost yelling. "What am I supposed to think. The tracks led us within a mile of Garrett's house. Where else would the man have come from?"

"Garrett ain't no back-shooter, Blaine, and you know it." The sheriff's face was redder than ever. He stood up at the table.

"Sit back down, O'Riley and calm yourself. I know old Mason Garrett's reputation better than that. You're perfectly right, it's plain he's no back shooter. But you tell me what's to keep Rafe Willis or one of those gunmen he calls cowboys from being the bushwhacker?"

"They're Mason Garrett's men, not Willis's. He'd never order anybody shot in the back."

"Rafe Willis would, and you know it. He's giving the orders over there now and you know that too. Don't tell me you think Willis wouldn't act on his own and hide it from Garrett."

"Mason Garrett would take that bullwhip of his to him and run him off his ranch, if he didn't shoot him for trying such a thing."

"Garrett might try, but do you really think he could stop him? Rafe Willis is more than a match for Garrett with a handgun and he's at least thirty years younger than the old man. It could be that Garrett's got a mountain lion by its tail in that foreman of his. Have you thought about that?"

O'Riley shook his head as Blaine continued, "I know Garrett wants Silver Creek Ranch. He's made no bones about it. He needs the water badly, but I've come to believe that he's not the man to do the things that have been happening here. I do believe though, that Rafe Willis is. In fact, I believe he could do almost anything if it would benefit him in some way."

"Rafe Willis is a hard man, that a fact," O'Riley said. "He's got rid of all of Garrett's old riders and brought in a bunch of men that can only be called riff-raff and hardcases. Maybe he's being too free with Garrett's orders. I'll ride over there later today and see what Willis has to say. I ain't accusing anybody over there of anything, mind you. I'm just asking."

"I didn't really expect you to do that much," Blaine said sarcastically.

"I do my job, Blaine." O'Riley's voice shook with anger. "You can't accuse people of such things as have been going on around here without no evidence. Garrett's a respected rancher in these parts. He's been here a sight longer than you have, too, maybe you should remember that."

"What in blazes is that supposed to mean?" Blaine glared at the sheriff as he straightened up and crossed his arms.

"Not a darn thing." O'Riley jumped up and grabbed his hat. "I'll send Del back to tell you if I find out anything."

The sheriff stomped through the house to the front door. Del Ketchum got up from the table, nodded to Blaine, and followed the sheriff without speaking. As they passed through the front room the men thanked Julie Blaine for the meal and her hospitality.

Julie Blaine entered the kitchen and said. "Russ, you've lost all your manners. Those men were guests at our table."

Blaine stared at her disapproving face. "Don't tell me my business, wife," he snapped. Gasping at his uncharacteristic rudeness, Julie stared as he turned and stomped out, slamming the back door.

Andrea came into the room to find her mother sitting at the table sobbing. Her head lay on her folded arms, hiding her face. "I heard the way Daddy spoke to you, Mama. You know he didn't mean that. He's just upset to death about everything that's happened."

She slipped her arm around her mother's shoulders. "Don't cry, Mama, please. You know Daddy didn't mean to hurt your feelings."

Julie dried her face with her apron. "He makes me so mad. The nerve of him. Roaring at me like that. Telling me to mind my own business. I've worked as hard as he has to make a home out of this ranch."

"Hush, Mama. Daddy will be back in here in a few minutes begging your forgiveness. You know that."

"Humph." Julie straightened her shoulders, her eyes bright with angry tears. "Let him beg. The big bully. I may never speak to him again."

Andrea smiled ruefully as she went outdoors. Her mother and father were close and usually discussed everything and made every decision together. But they were flint and steel when they disagreed. She knew from experience that the house would be unbearable for a few days until they made up.

Daddy's scared, Andrea thought as she walked to the corral. *He's worried about us all and it makes him touchy. Mama will sure make him pay for what he said.* She chuckled to herself as she strode along. She was dressed in her usual outfit of worn jeans and loose jacket. She carried her hat in her hand. Her gleaming brown curls bounced on her shoulders.

"Hey there, ma'am." Nelson Ames came out of the bunkhouse and called to her. He stepped into her path and waited until she stopped a few feet in front of him. Smiling, he said, "I thought you were a mighty pretty boy when I first saw you, but I see now that you must be Billy's little sister, Andrea."

The young man's face was even more pleasant than it had appeared when she peeped at him out of her window the evening before. Andrea couldn't help smiling in response to his friendly grin. "You're right. I'm Andrea Blaine, and you're Nelson Ames."

"Well, now. You actually know who I am. I'm downright

flattered," he said, adding, "Pants and all, you're sure the prettiest girl I ever saw."

Andrea laughed. "Don't bother offering me left-handed compliments, Mr. Ames. I'm perfectly used to cowboys' foolishness, and you're obviously just like every other cowboy I ever met."

"Oh, now. That's an awful way to talk. Why, you and me are almost kin, our Dads are such good friends."

Andrea called back over her shoulder as she walked around him and into the barn. "I'll see you later then, cousin."

Nelson stopped grinning and looked astonished. He turned around and yelled at Andrea's back. "I didn't mean that."

Andrea hurried on to Pat's stall, ignoring the brash young man. Another face filled her mind as she saddled and bridled her pony. Nelson Ames smiling face seemed terribly young. When she placed her image of him beside that of her image of the hard planes of Kyle Turner's face Nelson Ames's face seemed to be unformed. Ames' cheerful eyes and big, friendly grin reminded her of a happy puppy. Kyle Turner's face seemed to have been hardened by sadness and perhaps by violence. His blue eyes held a steely strength. Every time she thought of the way he looked after he had shaved off his beard her heart began to pound.

The ride to the north end of the valley was always Andrea's greatest pleasure. She loved nothing better than to be out early, riding the open range as her world woke up to a new day. She held Pat down to an easy canter so she could enjoy the ride. This morning her thoughts were in turmoil.

"I must be losing my mind," she muttered to herself. "All I want is be where I can look at that man. Drat, he thinks of me as a kid." Her face flamed when she remembered the humiliation of having to tell him she wasn't the young boy he had assumed her to be.

Hmmm—maybe I'll wear my blue riding skirt and a

white blouse the next time I ride up to the cabin. He might notice I'm not a boy or a kid any more if he sees me dressed like that. She spent the rest of the ride plotting ways she could get Kyle Turner to notice that she was a grown up woman. She was thinking so intently that she was in the edge of the trees before she realized it.

"Easy, Pat, slow down now," she said. Leaning over to pat the pony's neck and pulling the reins to slow him to a walk," she continued. "You might slip and get hurt if you take this path too fast."

John was bringing a bucket full of fresh water down the path from the spring when Andrea rode into the clearing. "Good morning, little girl," and waved as he went into the cabin with the bucket.

"Little girl, huh." Andrea muttered. "So much for you, Andrea." She turned Pat loose to graze in the little clearing by the spring and stomped back down the path to the cabin.

"There's not much need of asking how you are feeling this morning," she said, smiling. "You made it to the spring and back, so you must be mending fast."

"I needed the exercise and I wanted to check on my horse. Prince is used to being groomed and fed every day, I didn't want him to get lonesome and leave. Those hobbles you fixed wouldn't hold him if he decided he wanted to be somewhere else."

John was on his knees in front of the fireplace, lighting the fire. He turned to look at Andrea and said, "I'm simply starved. I've got to find another place to hole up in a day or too. I'd like to be able to cook up something whenever I get hungry."

"I thought you planned to stay here a few more days." Andrea heard the slight note of fear in her own voice. She didn't want him to leave.

John stood up and stretched his long arms. He walked over to her. "I'm going to stay around here close for awhile. I planned to spend a week or two hunting. I've been thinking about your father's trouble. I might be able to find out something to help if no one else knows I'm here."

"The people who are doing this to us shoot people, re-member?" Andrea asked as her eyebrows raised. "My fa-ther's riders are more than a little crazy with worry. Someone is liable to shoot you again if you try to sneak around here. You simply have to openly belong to one side or the other. If you go poking around the valley or over to Garrett's ranch each side will think you're a spy for the other side or they might even think you're the bushwhacker that killed Chuck Holden. You'll get killed." Andrea's voice was full of distress.

"Calm down, honey. I'm not going to get killed." John placed his hands on Andrea's shoulders and smiled down at her as he asked, "Can you trust me enough to keep my presence here a secret for a few more days?"

Andrea looked steadily into his eyes. She was struggling to keep frightened tears from starting. "I think you know I trust you. I don't know why I should, you're not exactly open about yourself and you haven't explained why you're even here, but I know I can trust you not to hurt me or my family."

"Good girl," John said as he leaned over and kissed her lightly on her nose. "I'll not abuse your trust, Andrea, and I thank you for it."

Andrea felt herself tremble at his nearness. Her tears were under control now, and she was beginning to feel angry at being treated like a child. She shook her shoulders free of John's hands and walked over to snatch the frying pan up from the table. "I'd better cook up some extra food for you to carry," she said through clenched teeth as she began to hack slices from the piece of bacon.

John's eyebrow's shot up at the tone of her voice and the way she was attacking the bacon. "What's the matter with you?" he demanded.

"Nothing, nothing at all," Andrea said angrily, keeping her back to him as she worked.

She suddenly realized how irrational she sounded and her voice softened to its usual friendliness again. "It just scares me for people to get shot. You're taking an awful chance just being here. Our riders are so jumpy they might shoot first and talk later. I don't want you to get killed like Chuck Holden did." She lowered her head and hid her red face as she adjusted the pan of bacon on the fire.

"I'll skulk around and hide behind trees like an Indian." John chuckled at the picture of himself sneaking about. "Will you promise to meet me back here in say, four days? I'll come to your ranch if I can, but if I don't show up at your door in three days will you come up here to the cabin the next day?"

"You're leaving today?" Andrea stood up.

"I thought I might slip out about dark. I climbed up to your lookout for a while yesterday. I think I've got the layout of the valley pretty well fixed in my mind. Can a horse get over the rim near that lightening-blasted pine that's almost directly across the valley from here?"

"As a matter of fact," Andrea answered, "that cut takes you straight over to Mason Garrett's ranch." Suddenly she felt uneasy. She couldn't help but question her judgment about this man. How did he happen to pick the route to Garrett's place so easily? Was she making a bad mistake to trust him?

"Is there good enough cover to get close to the Garrett ranch buildings without me being seen?" John asked.

"There's plenty of cover all the way. There are rocks as you come down the slope, then trees and an open space for more than a mile. Then you enter those big pines. You not only can't be seen once you get in there, its almost impossible to track anyone on that thick bed of pine needles. The main ranch buildings and the house sit beyond the grove of pines. If you wait to go after full dark you could get to the buildings easily without being seen."

"Would you mind telling me what you are planning to do?" Andrea tried to keep her voice normal, but she couldn't stop sounding concerned.

John sat down at the table. "I'm not exactly sure what I'll do yet. I thought that if I could hear some talk over there, maybe I might get a clue as to what Garrett or Willis or their men are really up to."

"That's plain enough for anybody to see. Garrett plans on getting our ranch and our water. He's tried to buy it and couldn't, so he's going to run us off to get it." Andrea's words were bitter.

"I noticed the creek today. It looks like a lot of water. Didn't Garrett or Hostetter own land where the creek leaves the valley?"

"It doesn't leave. It meanders around from here to the other side of the valley floor then disappears into a cavern in the mountain. It forms an underground river. You can hear the water roaring through under the rock. It's just swallowed up and never comes back to the surface.

"The place has always fascinated me. Alec Gunnison told us that the Indians used to call the whole valley and especially the place where the creek disappears 'Death Water.' It was a religious place for them."

"Death Water. It sounds almost frightening when you say it like that." John thought about the story for a moment then repeated Andrea's words aloud, "The creek forms an underground river."

"Say," he asked, "can you get inside the mountain to see the place where the water disappears?"

"Alec Gunnison claimed he'd been in the cavern. There's a place you could climb in, but it's real scary. One slip and it's no telling where you'd end up. The Indians thought you'd go to another world where you'd wander around lost forever."

Andrea shuddered and wrapped her hands around her arms as she talked. "It makes me cold to even talk about it."

John smiled at her across the table. "Will you take me to see the cavern someday?"

Andrea's heart flip-flopped. She caught her breath and said, "That would be nice." She smiled back at him.

Oh, no, she thought. His voice was rough and soft at the same time. It seemed to reach out and touch her. Andrea jumped up from the table and busied herself packing some food for him. Her hands trembled as she tied a clean cloth around several pieces of bacon wrapped in slices of bread.

Her reactions to this man were beginning to frighten her. He was a stranger. Her intuition told her he was not being completely truthful with her. He had carefully led any conversation away from himself and encouraged her to give him information about the area and the people in it.

Strangest of all, he appeared especially interested in the problems her father had experienced while protecting their ranch. Now he had made it clear that the first place he wanted to head for was the Double G ranch. To the source of all the Blaine family's troubles. Sometimes it was hard to believe that the only reason he came here was to spend some time hunting and fishing.

Andrea knew she should be on her guard against a man who arrived in the area the way this one had. He had been running from a sheriff, and was wounded while he was escaping, by his own admission. She had only his word that he was in the right and the sheriff was a crook. Andrea sighed. There was no explaining her reactions, but somehow she just trusted Kyle Turner, whatever he had done. Whatever he was planning.

John was filled with impatience at his continued weakness. He had come back home with a confused idea of helping his father. Now he was planning to try to stop him from trying to push the Blaines off their ranch. That is if he could determine that his father really was really responsible for their trouble. He had been riding for Ned Wilson's ranch near El Paso. He had spent two years building a reputation as a steady dependable hand and Wilson had recently made him his foreman. He was out on the range when Alec Gunnison came to the ranch looking for him.

Gunnison had been John's friend and neighbor once. It was Alec who had taught him to hunt, read sign, and live on what nature provided. There was a time when the boy had tagged after Gunnison every minute he could. Even after he had become a man, with a man's job of running his father's ranch, he had made time to visit the Gunnison cabin regularly.

Alec had taught him to use a handgun. The old man had been so fast before his hands had gotten gnarled and twisted from using a pick digging for gold, that as a young boy John was amazed to watch the man draw. He had patiently taught John the motions. The draw he used seemed awkward at first but with practice it grew into the fluid movement that placed a gun in his hand almost without conscious thought. He had given John the Navy Colt he wore and taught him a skill that had saved his life several times in the years since he left home.

When Alec came to Wilson's place in El Paso, he waited for John on the bunkhouse porch. Leaning against the log wall, he looked only a little drier and grayer than when John Garrett left home. As John approached the bunkhouse, he straightened up to hold out his hand. "Well, son, you're sure a welcome sight for these old eyes."

"Alec." John grasped his hand in both of his. Smiling into the old man's faded blue eyes, he asked, "What in the world are you doing here?"

"I'm just passing through, son, but I wanted to bring you a message. You're needed at home."

"What's happened? What do you mean? How am I needed there?" John's concern was mixed with wariness and a little bitterness.

"Calm down now. I ain't exactly straight on what's happening myself. But your pa's been pushing hard to get hold of Silver Creek Ranch for one thing."

"I'd heard that years ago, Alec. In fact he used to talk about all the big things he could do if only he had that water. He was put out with you because you wouldn't sell to him."

"Yeah, but either your pa's mighty changed or his foreman, that Rafe Willis he hired a couple of years ago, is playing his own hand. Right soon after you left home, Johnny, I sold my valley to a settler named Blaine that come here from somewheres out east. I think Blaine came from Georgia or one of the old Southern states."

"I figured it might calm things down some for me to sell to a stranger, but a couple of years after I left, Tim Hostetter lost some cattle, then he got back-shot out on his range one night. Now lately, Blaine's begun to lose cattle regular. Worse than that, now there's been some more back shooting. One of Blaine's riders was injured."

John looked puzzled. "Alec, you surely don't think my father would do that, do you?"

"I surely don't want to think such a thing, Johnny, but there's other folks willing to believe it. The Double G needs that water to expand. Anyone can see that on the surface. You can remember how hard your Pa pushed me to sell him my place. He's pushed some of his cows over onto the Hostetter place now, but it's almost as dry as the Double G."

"There's water enough on the Double G if Pa has Hostetter's ranch. That big pool over there never goes dry."

"Talk is that there's upwards of 20,000 head of cows on the Double G. There ain't enough water there for that many cows. Cattle prices are going up every year. Your pa always did think big. Then there's the way he got the use of Hostetter's place to make a man think. Folks have started questioning the circumstances of that shooting."

"What exactly happened to Hostetter?" John asked apprehensively.

"Hostetter was killed by two .44 slugs in his back. His wife allowed it must have been rustlers. He'd been complaining of losing cows and had ridden out to check on his herd one night. He didn't show up at home the next morning. His wife took a couple of their riders out to search and they found him, lying on his face in the mud. That killing ain't never been explained. That's set people to wondering, and now Blaine's rider's been injured. He was shot from ambush just like Hostetter was. He was lucky not to have been killed."

"My God, Alec. I don't know what to think or do. I

swore I'd never put my foot on the ranch again and Pa said he'd shoot me if I ever tried."

"Your pa's getting older, son. He needs help whether he wants it or not. I've been trailing you for weeks cause I felt like you ought to know about it.

"There's something else you need to know too, boy. Your daddy never said it, but I think he somehow found out that I had found that piddling little bit of gold back up where Silver Creek gets lost under the mountain. I figure that might be part of the reason for this trouble.

"It could be the assayer over to Smithville got drunk and talked some, I don't know how anybody could have found out. It could be that someone found my diggings when they were out hunting. I'm afraid that gold could be the real reason your pa had for pushing me so hard to buy my place. It's the reason you could never understand what he did, and it sort of makes it my fault that you and your pa fell out."

"I'll be darn if it's your fault. Gold or no gold, he had no call to try to take a bullwhip to me, even if I did tell him to let you alone about selling your place. When I told him I wouldn't stand for some of his ideas about how to get hold of your place, he got so mad he grabbed up that big bullwhip he always carries. I had to hit him or go for my gun. I wasn't going to stand there and let him whip me." John's voice was thick. All the anger he had felt when his father raised the whip to hit him flared through him as he recalled the incident.

"I've felt responsible for the break between you and your pa, son. You need to go home and patch things up with the old man. He's getting along in years and he's got nobody else.

"It could be that your pa hasn't done anything wrong. I been sort of suspecting that Willis is holding something over your pa's head to control him. You've got a duty to go home and find out what's happening. That's why I chased around over half the Texas desert to find you."

"How in the world did you ever find me? I thought by

using Granddad Turner's name I could just disappear."
John looked chagrined.

Alec laughed as he said, "It won't no big trick to find
you. First, I knew your Granddad Turner, and I figured that
was a name you might use. Second, there ain't five men in
the country that can shoot like you can and folks love to
talk. Finally, you're working on the ranch of one of the
men I rode with in the Rangers years ago. Where else
would you go except to somebody I had mentioned to you."

"Blast, people are a pain in the butt," John said in disgust.

"Don't talk like a fool, boy. You better be thankful
you're good with that gun, you're liable to need it if you're
going to help your pa."

"Well, I'm not thankful. Somebody's always got something to prove. When a man gets a reputation with a gun
he's set apart from everybody else and has to watch every
step he makes. There's always some ranny that thinks he
can kill you for your reputation. And besides that, Pa ordered me to get off the ranch and said if I ever came back
he would shoot me."

"Ain't nobody killed you yet, and you know that your
pa would never shoot you. The old man was just mad,
exactly like you was, and you both said a whole lot more
than you meant and you know it. Git on your horse and go
home, Johnny. No matter what yore pa said or did you owe
him a duty to help him if there's any way you can."

"He wouldn't accept my help, Alec." John turned away
to pace up and down the porch floor.

"He don't have to know. Go around the back way to my
cabin. Maybe you can find out the whole story before anybody knows you're around."

"I'll think about it, Alec. I'm obliged to you for looking
me up." John looked down at the floor as he spoke.

"Don't you go all stiff and proud like your pa does,
Johnny. You've got to go. I've cleared it with Wilson, so
you can leave here right away. You should stay to home

when you get there, but if you don't, Wilson will welcome you back here anytime you want a job."

John had no answer for that. He shook hands with his old friend and thoughtfully watched him mount his horse and ride out of sight down the lane. His father mixed up in shootings from ambush and cattle theft. He shook his head in puzzlement. It all seemed impossible.

Tossing and turning in his bunk all that night John wrestled with his anger against his father. It was still deep and raw even after six years. The old man had tried to shame him in front of their cowboys by hitting him with a bullwhip. He couldn't have just stood there and taken it.

Throughout a sleepless night John had never considered the possibility of not going home to find out what was going on, but he fervently wished there were no need for it. He thought he had put it all behind him, and now all the old wounds seemed fresh. He still felt his father had a lot to answer for.

It was almost dark when John left the cabin. He carried his Henry in his good hand and walked his horse at a steady pace. He was riding Prince bareback. The big Spanish saddle was much too heavy for him to handle with only one good arm. He rode under the bank in front of the cabin, then down toward the valley floor at a point out of sight of the Blaine's house. He constantly felt his weakness and knew he had to conserve his strength.

When he finally reached the level, he rode straight across the valley toward the lightning-blasted pine he had marked as his guide. The valley was quiet except for the occasional lowing of cattle in the distance. He could see lights in the house and other ranch buildings. He stopped every few minutes to listen and scan the shadowy hills for signs of movement.

The horse had to wade the creek twice as he made his way across the range. When he approached Blaine's cattle he detoured around them to the eastern side of the valley. He didn't want to run across any of the Blaine riders standing guard. The moon was high up and bright, but by staying close to the hills or in the edge of the trees whenever possible, he made it across without anyone noticing him. He chuckled to think how displeased Blaine would be to know how easy it was.

When he reached the far slope, John stopped to rest before starting up the hill. He dismounted and seated himself on the ground where he could lean back against a boulder. "Shucks," he muttered, closing his eyes for a few moments. "I'm too weak for this." He rubbed his healing shoulder to help loosen the muscles.

The night was bright. A pale moon was well up above the hills behind his shoulder. John rested his head against his knees for a few minutes, then stood up and started up the slope. He walked and led his horse. He could remember climbing this path on foot and carrying a rifle so many times as he went back and forth to Alec's cabin. The familiarity in every boulder and tree, even every shadow, made him feel strange. It seemed that even the land was watching his every step.

John had to stop to rest again when he reached the crest of the hill. *Maybe I've taken on too much,* he thought as he pulled deep breaths into his aching lungs. *I won't accomplish anything if I can't make it back to the other side of the valley before morning.*

His wounded shoulder was pounding with pain when he got to his feet again, but he was delighted to realize that he wasn't as tired as he had expected to be. He was slowly regaining his strength. Dragging himself up on Prince's back he pushed doggedly on, keeping his pace a steady but fast walk.

As soon as he came out of the rocks and reached the level range he began to make better time. He didn't have to worry about anyone hearing the horse now. The ground he was riding over was covered in the stubble of short grass. It was evident that cattle had been grazing here in the last few days. There was good footing for Prince. He could hear the occasional lowing of cattle a long way ahead. The sounds grew louder as he approached the grove of pines.

No wonder Blaine's men lost the trail here. The entire area under the big pines was covered in a thick carpet of fallen needles. John realized he couldn't even hear his horse's hooves striking the ground. When he came to the edge of the pines nearest the Double G the moon was bright enough to see the buildings clearly.

The ranch looked much like it had when he left it six years before. Nothing about the buildings or fences appeared to be changed. The only difference he could see from this position was that there were many more horses in the corral than he could ever remember seeing.

John sat his horse a few minutes to stare at the ranch spread out before him, slowly taking in the beauty of the scene in the bright moonlight. The ranch house was gleaming white. There were lights in two front windows on the ground floor. That would be his father's office. The bunkhouse blazed with lights.

He had forgotten how much he loved this ranch. He had planned to improve their herd of cattle gradually by cross breeding with Shorthorns. That way, he knew they could make a good living and still run no more cows than their water and grass could easily support. He felt a wave of bitterness in his chest when he thought of the years that had passed since his dream died.

Tying Prince's reins to a tree in the edge of the woods where he wouldn't be seen even if someone came close, John took a straight path to the corrals on foot. He walked slowly, conserving his strength and hoping no one would see him. He knew he probably couldn't run to save his life.

As he walked along beside the fence and buildings, John began to notice that the fence was broken and patched in several places rather than repaired, as it should have been. There was trash thrown against the side of the barn, and cans and paper scattered about on the ground. The door to the smokehouse stood open. It was empty. He realized the whole place was looking run down and neglected. It was a

mystery how there could be so many more men than usual
working on the ranch, but the place could look as though
no one was taking care of it. Keeping low, he moved along
beside the corral fence, passed the barn and the other out-
buildings, and crossed the open space to the side of the
bunkhouse.

Lights were blazing in the main room of the building
where the riders lived and slept. John crept up beside a
back window. Keeping to the side so he couldn't be seen,
he looked in. He quickly counted eighteen riders in the big
room. It was evident by the number of bunks made up for
use that more men lived there. Probably some were out
riding night guard around the herd.

Most of the men were crowded around two large tables
in the center of the room playing cards. Whiskey bottles
sat on the tables and the men were talking and laughing
loudly. Several more men were lying down in their bunks.
A few of those men were reading, but others seemed to be
sleeping, in spite of all the noise made by the crowd of
half-drunken men in the middle of the room.

John shook his head when he saw the whiskey bottles
sitting openly on the tables. His father had always had an
ironclad rule against a rider that worked for him drinking
in the bunkhouse or anywhere else on the Double G. He
had seen him throw good men off the place for breaking
that rule. There was something really wrong here, something that needed explaining.

Just as he was turning away from the window, John noticed that the door to the foreman's room at the back of
the bunkhouse was open, but the room was empty. He
could see that the cot was stripped and the bare mattress
was rolled up and tied, indicating that the bed was not in
use.

That's darned odd, he thought. *The foreman always slept
in that room, except when I was foreman.* A crazy thought
came to him. *Could that Willis guy be sleeping in the ranch
house?*

If Willis was sleeping in the house, something was terribly wrong with his father. Mason Garrett was so conscious of his position as owner of the Double G, he would never let a hired man sleep in the house, even it he was the foreman. Either he was ill and didn't know what was going on, or the foreman was forcing the old man to let him to do what he wanted.

John knew the moon was entirely too bright for him to approach the house and try to find out anything more. He was fairly safe from detection as long as he stayed close to the bunkhouse. The men were making so much noise with their card game the only way they would know he was there would be to see him. But if his father or Willis should happen to hear him as he tried to approach the house, he would probably be caught, and that would put paid to any chance he had of finding an explanation for the crazy things that were happening.

John shook his head when he thought of the riders sitting around the table in the bunkhouse playing cards. Men who did the kind of work the ranch required couldn't sit up late and play cards and drink, except maybe on Saturday night. Any man who did a full days' work riding herd, mending fence, and all the other things that had to be done would be worn out so badly he would be glad to get into his bunk most nights. These men were just the kind he was afraid he might find here. They certainly bore out what old Alec Gunnison told him. The men definitely looked and acted more like gunfighters than cowboys.

Moving back from the side of the bunkhouse, John retraced his steps away from the lights of the bunkhouse, around the other buildings, and across the pasture. Untying Prince, he mounted and headed back through the woods toward Silver Creek. He mused as he rode on what he could do next. He felt anxious about his father. He might be mad at the old man, but he didn't want anything to happen to him. He actually felt a little guilty leaving the ranch, but there was nothing he could do until he learned more about the situation.

By the time he dismounted to lead Prince down the narrow trail to the valley floor, John had made up his mind. He would have to sneak into town and talk to some people. Their banker was probably the best man for him to go to. He might be able to shed some light on what was happening. He would ask him to keep his presence in Hinton a secret. It might be good if he could stay a stranger named Kyle Turner for a little while longer.

It would also help if he could find one or two of Hostetter's old outfit and question them about the circumstances surrounding Hostetter's killing. That seemed to be the beginning of the trouble in the valley, and one of Hostetter's riders might have some thoughts about who might have killed his boss.

I don't know how Hostetter's killing fits in with what's happening now, or how whatever I find out might implicate Pa, John thought, *but I have to know. I just have to know.*

After hobbling Prince and leaving him in the clearing to graze, John flopped down on his stomach by the spring to drink his fill of the icy water. He was so exhausted he lay there and rested almost an hour before he felt strong enough to walk the few yards down hill to the cabin door. Once inside, he wolfed down two pieces of the cold bacon wrapped in the last of his bread, and lay down on the bunk to immediately fall asleep.

Chapter Six

It was barely light the next morning when John heard Andrea's horse moving through the pines behind the cabin. She rode the pony around to the cabin instead of turning him loose in the clearing to graze. That was a clear sign that she didn't plan to stay long. He sat on the doorstep and watched her dismount and turn to face him.

"Good morning," he said. "You're out early, aren't you?"

Andrea had taken her hat off and stuck it over the horn of her saddle. Her hair was tangled around her face. Suddenly, he saw that she was beautiful. Her face was a perfect oval, and her lips were pink and soft-looking. John drew in his breath and dropped his head as he felt his face getting red.

"It's not so early," she answered. "I woke up, so I thought I'd ride up on the mesa today and see if I can spot anything going on. You're out early, though. I thought you were going to rest to get your strength back."

"I'm rested. Come on in and I'll start a fire so we can have some coffee. I want to talk to you."

Wondering at his serious tone, Andrea followed him into the cabin and began to prepare the coffee. When the fire was blazing and the pot was nestled against two logs to heat, they sat down at the table.

Andrea looked questioningly at John's face and asked, "I thought you might be gone when I got here. Are you planning to leave today?"

"That's part of it. I went across the valley and up to the Double G buildings last night. There were a couple of times that I got so weak and tired I thought I wouldn't make it there or back, but here I am."

"I'm amazed you had the strength," Andrea exclaimed.

"It was actually better than I expected. And I feel much stronger this morning. I believe the exercise helped me."

"Did you find out anything at all?" she asked.

"I saw some things that struck me as strange, but I didn't learn much," John said, shaking his head.

"What is it you expect to find out by nosing around Garrett's place?"

"I'm not sure. I did learn a couple of things that match the talk your father's been hearing. Garrett does have a crew of hard cases working for him, that's true enough. It looks as though there may be close to thirty of them. I sneaked up to a bunkhouse window and watched them for a while. They don't act like working cowboys. They were sitting up around a table after dark, playing cards and drinking."

"I can't really tell Dad anything like that until I can tell him about you."

"You can tell him the whole story when you get back to the house tonight. I'm leaving here today. I have to find a safe place to camp, where a small fire won't be seen. I'll go on over to Garrett's ranch again tomorrow night. Maybe I'll find out something useful."

Andrea was obviously shaken. "When will I see you again?"

"I'll come to your ranch in a few days. I'll come right up to the front door as bold as brass with a good story to tell," John said with a grin.

"I thought you were afraid that someone would give you away to the sheriff that was chasing you," Andrea said in a unusually harsh tone. There was almost a sneer in her voice.

"I'm strong enough to take care of myself now. I just needed to hide until I could heal a little."

"I'm sorry. I guess I'm disappointed that you're leaving," the girl said, hanging her head. "This has been an adventure for me. I'll miss you."

John's eyes met hers. "I'll miss you, Andrea," he said softly. "I'll be back, sooner than you think."

"Where will you go?"

"I'm not sure yet. I'll ride around a little to get the lay of the land, and I'll find a good place. I'm used to lying out at night. I plan to go well out of the valley to make my camp. I'll also be careful to avoid any of Garrett's riders. I don't want to have to explain what I'm doing nosing around, as you say, to either side of this ruckus until I know more about what's going on.

"Andrea," he asked, "will you tell your father about helping me when you get home tonight?"

Andrea thought for a minute. "I think that's the best thing for me to do. He'll yell and scream for a few minutes, but if you're already gone there's not much he'll be able to do about it."

"You're sure you won't be punished or anything?" John asked. His look was so intent, and appeared so concerned, that Andrea felt herself blushing under his gaze.

"I'm not worried about my father," she answered. "It's my mother who will be truly upset. She's already having a fit because I still dress in pants and ride astride and roam around in the woods. If she had her way, I'd already be safely married with a couple of babies to keep me at home."

Andrea looked so chagrined as she spoke that John laughed aloud. "What will you do when I come to the ranch? Must I pretend I don't know you?"

"Please stop laughing at me. I'll tell Daddy about you first, and he'll help me make it right with Mother. I'll just have to stay at the house and wear dresses for a few days until she calms down.'

Standing up from her chair, Andrea held her hand to John. She stared into his face. Would this be the last time she would ever see him?

When she found words, she spoke formally, and her voice trembled slightly. "I'll say good-bye for now, then. I'll look for you at Silver Creek in a few days."

John caught her hand in both of his and looked down into her eyes. His voice sounded hoarse as he almost whispered, "I'll miss seeing you every day, but I'll be at the ranch in no more than three days. I promise, Andrea."

The girl continued to stare into his eyes for a moment, then she turned and left the cabin, not looking back. A moment later John heard the pounding of her pony's hooves as she recklessly let him run down the crooked trail toward the ranch. She wasn't going to leave her horse in the area near the spring as she usually did. He couldn't blame her. She had no way of knowing for sure that he would show up at the Blaine ranch as he promised. She might think he was lying and didn't want to take a chance of running in to him when he went to the clearing for his horse.

It didn't take long for John to pack up his gear and be ready to ride. He left most of the items Andrea had brought to make him comfortable sitting on the table. He had the small fry pan and coffeepot he always carried in his pack. He pulled the door of the cabin tight to keep animals from getting inside. Leaving his gear on the step, he took his bridle and went to the clearing to get Prince.

He held the horse to a walk and followed the path downhill almost to the edge of the forest, then turned to the east. He kept the edge of the pines in view, but stayed well back where the tall ponderosa pine canopy had shaded out all of the brush and small trees and the forest floor was clear enough to make riding comfortable. After heading east for close to an hour, John came to a small trickle of water that ran straight down through the woods to the valley floor. He crossed the brook and turned the horse north to ride straight uphill.

Following the trickle of water, he pushed Prince along the faint track as far as he could ride, then dismounted and continued uphill, leading the horse. Finally the land leveled off at an opening in the trees. At the edge of the glade a small spring fed the brook. John removed the bit from Prince's mouth so he could graze and drink, but left his saddle in place. He cupped his hands and drank from the spring, then sat down under a large tree to rest.

Refreshed, he watered Prince again before he remounted. Following a game trail that edged across the slope to the east he continued to angle up toward the rim. The path finally leveled out on a tiny mesa. The flat place was no more than six feet wide. It ran along the escarpment for several hundred feet, then entered a group of large rocks. As he approached a wall that appeared to be a dead end, John entered an opening that looked to be no more than a fold in the rocks. He had exited and entered the valley many times by this route, but by the looks of things, none of the Blaine riders had discovered it, not even Andrea. It was a possible way for someone to get a few cows out of the valley.

He had to dismount and tie his stirrups up on the saddle before leading Prince along the narrow trail that twisted and turned through the rocks to come out among a growth of mesquite that completely obscured the opening. Once clear of the worst of the mesquite, John re-mounted and pushed his horse to a trot. He worked his way through the scattered scrub and brush, stopping to rest several times. Finally, he reached the road where he could let the horse run. He knew he was taking a real chance on meeting someone who would recognize him, riding out in the open this way, but it was the quickest way to Hinton, and he wanted to reach the town just after dark.

Lamplight glowed from windows here and there as he passed outlying houses on the approach to the town. John turned from the road before it became the main street, and walked his horse along the alley that ran in back of the commercial buildings. When he came to a large house beside the bank, he dismounted and dropped the reins to ground hitch Prince. He let himself in at a gate in the wooden fence that enclosed the back yard, and walked to the door.

John knew Asa Hamilton would recognize him instantly, but he wanted to make sure there was no one in the house except the banker and his wife before he knocked. Lights were burning in the kitchen and in the dining room beyond. John peered through the glass in the door. He could see the couple sitting at the table eating. They seemed to be alone.

Mrs. Hamilton rose from the table and entered the kitchen with a large bowl in her hands. John tapped on the door to get her attention. She placed the bowl on a cabinet and crossed the room to open the door. "May I help you, young man?" she asked.

"I'm sorry to bother you, ma'am," John said, holding his hat in his hand. "I'd like to speak to Mr. Hamilton if I may. It's important."

"We were just having our supper, couldn't you come to the bank tomorrow?" she asked as her husband reached her side and stared at the young man at the door.

"I'll talk to Johnny, Emily," he said, reaching to open the screen door. "Come on in son, what in the world are you doing here? I'm astonished. You were the last person I expected to see."

"I need to talk to you about my father, Mr. Hamilton. I can wait out here on the porch until you and your wife finish your supper."

"You'll do nothing of the kind. Come on in the house."

Turning to his wife, the banker said, "Set another place, Emily. I can see from his dusty clothes that this boy has had a long ride, and he's bound to be hungry." He led John into the dining room and motioned for him to take a chair at the table.

John wondered at the banker's excessive friendliness. He didn't remember that Hamilton had even liked him much before he left home, but he appeared to be overjoyed to see him for some strange reason. He decided to relax long enough to enjoy the hot meal spread before him.

As she served them plates of apple pie, John turned to his hostess. "Mrs. Hamilton, this is delicious. It's been a while since I sat at a table and ate a meal like this."

"Thank you, Mr. Garrett." She smiled proudly. "I like to see a man enjoy his food."

Hamilton placed his napkin beside his plate. "As soon as we finish eating we can go over to the bank and talk in my office, John. I'm anxious to know where you've been for almost six years."

John nodded in agreement, still thinking there was something strange here. He remembered that the last time he had been in the bank Hamilton had treated him as though he were no more than one of his father's hired hands, hardly worth the man's notice. The banker's behavior puzzled him. Why would he change? What could he want?

Thanking Mrs. Hamilton again for the meal, John followed Hamilton out the back door of the house and across the yard to the side door of the bank. The banker stopped to lock the outer door of the bank behind him as they entered directly into his private office. He lit the lamp on his desk and motioned for John to take a chair.

"Have a seat, John, and tell me how I can help you." He seated himself in a high-backed leather chair behind his desk and lit a cigar.

"I want to know what is going on at the Double G," John said. He thought the banker looked uncomfortable for a moment at his direct question, but the man smiled as he answered.

"I'm not sure I know everything that's going on, Johnny, but I've been concerned, and I'll tell you what I know. Your father hasn't been to town for more than two months. I'm always concerned when a good customer and a friend, as I have always considered your father, suddenly begins to act in strange ways."

"What do you mean, he's acting in strange ways?"

"I'm sure you know that for years your father has made a regular trip to town every month. His habit was to arrive just about the time the barbershop opened, get himself a shave and sometimes a haircut. Then he would go over to the mercantile and leave a list of supplies for them to get together for him. After that, he would go over to Maisie's Café, eat breakfast, and sit around drinking coffee and talking with his friends. Around ten o'clock he would come across the street and spend some time with Ted Bennett. He would leave Bennett's office about eleven, get his loaded wagon from the front of the mercantile, drive it around back of the hotel and park it, and disappear inside the hotel for the rest of the day."

John had to struggle not to laugh at the banker's description of his father's activities, but then he began to feel sort of sad and a little angry. His father would be livid to hear that this man had been watching his every step.

"What is it that you think is strange? Do you think my father could be ill or something like that?" John asked, beginning to feel impatient and a little aggravated.

"I honestly don't know what to think. Your father has been sending his foreman, Rafe Willis, in town with a note to take care of his business. I recognize your father's handwriting, so I've gone along with the things he instructed as long as they were just normal ones. Just regular pay for the hands and things like that.

"But this last week, Willis came in with a note from your father that directed me to sell the Hostetter place to Willis, and stating that he would stand good for the payment. Well, obviously I couldn't approve such a transaction as that without seeing your father in person. I sent Willis away. He was so furious I thought he would strike me when I refused him."

"That is strange, I've been told that my father had a crew over at Hostetter's ranch and had probably bought it."

"No, your father tried to buy the property, but after Hostetter was killed, and Mrs. Hostetter was ready to go back east, she directed me not to sell her ranch. She said she had a buyer for the place and as Bennett was her husband's lawyer he would handle all the legal matters. She refused to tell me anything more. I explained all that to your father almost two years ago. I've been to Bennett several times to try and find out if she actually sold the place and who the buyer is, but he won't tell me a thing.

"I know there are men living on the Hostetter place, but I don't think they're your father's men," the banker continued. "I heard someone was staying there from Russ Blaine's boy last week. After he was here I thought I should investigate. After all, I feel I at least owe Mrs. Hostetter that much. I rode out to there with a couple of men, and almost got my head shot off. We had almost reached the ranch house when suddenly rifle bullets started singing over our heads. We weren't prepared for that. None of us had long guns, so we turned our horses around and got out of there."

John shifted in his chair. He was more puzzled than ever. He wasn't sure why, but he suddenly felt he couldn't trust Hamilton. It was something about his voice. His words had a sort of hollow sound, as though the banker was listening to himself spin a tale. John watched the man's face as he kept on with the story.

"I haven't been to the sheriff about that yet. I've been trying to think what to do. I went directly over to Bennett's place when I got back to town and told him about it. He looked surprised, but he still wouldn't tell me anything. When I got back here to the bank I wrote a letter to Mrs. Hostetter, explaining what was happening and asking her to sell me the place or at least to give me written authority to go to the law about the matter. As it is, there really is little I can do except follow the instructions she gave me and leave protecting the property up to Bennett."

John shook his head as he stood up. "I'm not surprised you are puzzled, Mr. Hamilton. I certainly am. I think I'll hang around town and go to Bennett's office tomorrow. If he won't talk about this Hostetter ranch business maybe he'll tell me something to help me understand what's going on with my father. I want to find out as much as I can before I go out to the ranch."

John was sure he saw Hamilton's eyes change when he learned that he didn't plan to go to the Double G right away. "Be sure to tell your wife again how much I enjoyed that delicious meal, Mr. Hamilton." He stood up and started toward the door. "I'll come back by the bank in a few days and maybe I'll be able to let you know something."

"Don't be in such a hurry, John. I have an idea. I know you can take care of yourself. How about going out to the Hostetter place for me? You might be able to find out who those men are that shot at me. I would also like to know who's paying them and why they want to keep people away from there. I'll pay you for your time." Hamilton stubbed out his cigar and stood up from his chair to come around the desk and unlock the door.

"I'll have think about that and let you know later, Mr. Hamilton," John said as they left the office. "I want to see Bennett before I leave town."

"Will you stay at the hotel tonight?"

"Probably, I've been sleeping rough, and a bed would sure feel good."

"Well, think about my proposition, son. You look as though you could use a few dollars, and it would be a great service to me if you could at least find out who those men are out there."

John chuckled to himself as he walked back to his horse. The banker couldn't keep from revealing his contempt for anyone he viewed as a lesser personage. John knew he looked rough, and the banker had therefore pegged him as unimportant, even if he was Mason Garrett's only son. Hamilton was evidently betting that the big whipping incident had ended his relationship with his father. He obviously thought Garrett would turn his son away if he ever returned to the ranch. *Pa probably told him he had run me off and told me to never come back.*

Suddenly, the blow-up with his father didn't seem so important. He couldn't figure what was happening or where the different players fit, but there was something brewing, and him showing up in town had upset the banker for some reason.

As he walked his horse behind the buildings back toward the edge of town John heard a door shut. That was probably Hamilton going back to his house. Then caution inspired him to swiftly turn his horse between two buildings and cross the main street. He waited in the dark alley between the mercantile and the barbershop and watched the alley. A few minutes later he saw a horse and rider pass by headed the same the way he had been going.

Could Hamilton actually be following me? This could get interesting, he mused as he tried to identify the horseman in the darkness.

Going back across the street to the alley, John fell in behind the rider, keeping well back so he wouldn't hear him. The man followed the path around to the road and stopped for a moment as though he didn't know what to do. Finally, he turned away from town and let his horse run. The noise of the horses' hooves striking the hard dirt of the road covered any sound John made as he turned Prince into the open range. He walked the horse until he was out of earshot of anyone listening from the town, then urged him to a trot.

It was cold when John woke up. Starting up, he looked around almost guiltily. He hadn't meant to sleep. It was close to dawn. He had been so tired when he reached the clump of cottonwoods around a small creek he had stopped to rest for a few minutes. He was leaning back against the bole of a tree and his horse was ground hitched right beside him. He rubbed his face with his hands to wake himself up and went to the creek to get a drink and wash his face. Returning for the horse, he removed the bit from his mouth long enough for him to drink.

Mounted again, he kept on heading west. He knew that to continue the way he was headed would mean that he would cross a corner of his father's range. He hoped he

wouldn't be seen by one of the Double G riders. He would
be a stranger to most of them. The kind of men he had
seen living in the Double G bunkhouse might shoot first
and ask questions later.

John saw cows in the distance as he crossed a long
stretch of open range. He could see no horses with them.
They were a long way from the Double G ranch house, but
close enough to the little creek to find water. He remembered that there was a line shack nearby. He kept his horse
to a trot until he was back in some brushy woods where
he wasn't so exposed. The direction he was moving would
take him to Hostetter's place, but he had no intention of
riding up to the ranch house, not right away at any rate.

Later, John turned Prince to a northwesterly direction,
and followed along the edge of the hills where Alec Gunnison had found his gold mine. He guessed Alec had probably sold this area to Blaine along with Silver Creek.
Keeping Prince to a trot, he soon left Hostetter's range and
entered a dense pine forest. The day had warmed as it pro-
gressed, but it was cool under the trees.

Tired again and hungry, John pushed himself and the
horse to reach a safe camping place. *If I remember cor-
rectly,* he mused to himself, *I'm close to the caves up above
that hole where Silver Creek disappears underground.* He
had explored the labyrinth of caves high up above the pines
many times as a boy, and he knew there was at least one
of them where he and the horse could stay out of sight. He
would also be able to have a fire and if he kept it small,
its smoke wouldn't give away his location.

John could hear the water roaring as the creek entered
the hole in the earth several hundred feet below him and
nearer to the valley floor. He knew he was close to the
right place. Dismounting, he led Prince out of the trees.
Walking uphill and leading the horse, he soon he spotted
the rocky area where the cave's opening was. "Come on,
boy. We can hide up here and there's not much chance of
anyone finding us, except maybe Andrea. She's such an

Indian she probably knows her way around these caves better than I do."

Leading the horse up the rocky track, he moved slowly, periodically checking to make sure that Princes' shoes didn't leave marks on the stone that would give away his hiding place. Finally he entered a narrowing opening in the rocks. Turning a sharp corner, the passageway opened into a cavern that was like a huge room. Prince snorted his displeasure at the strange sound his hooves made striking the stone floor and echoing back from the walls of the cave.

"Take it easy, boy." John turned to stroke Prince's nose to calm him down, "Just a few more steps. You'll have a nice sandy place to rest. There's even a pool of water you'll be able to reach."

Dim light filtered into the cavern from a small opening in the roof. The narrow crack was high up and well hidden in the middle of a grove of aspens. The trees still held enough of their leaves to make it possible for him to have a small fire. There wouldn't be much chance of anyone noticing the smoke as it dissipated through the aspens.

Settling the horse in his makeshift stable John rubbed his back thoroughly with the saddle blanket. When he was finished, he dug a small bag of oats out of his saddlebag and fed them to the horse from his cupped hands. "I'll find you some more food, boy, but you've got plenty of water, and you won't starve for a day or two. I'm going to rest a few hours and then figure out what to do next." He continued to talk the entire time he was grooming the horse. The sound of John's voice calmed the big horse and he soon lost his nervousness and settled down.

As soon as the small fire had the tin frying pan hot, John dropped in four thick slices of bacon. While it was cooking he mixed some biscuit dough in the pan's up-turned top. When the bacon was done he set it aside to cool and dropped the bread dough into the sizzling grease, shaking the pan so it wouldn't stick. Turning the bread with his knife until it was well browned on both sides he sat the pan away from the fire for the food to cool enough for him eat.

He devoured the bread and bacon. Still hungry, he opened a can of peaches with the point of his knife and ate them, drinking the juice. Finally satisfied, John smothered his fire with some sand, and took the utensils to the pool to wash them before packing them back in his saddlebag.

It wasn't quite dark when John made his bed by spreading Prince's blanket on the soft sand at the back of the cave. Using his saddle for a pillow he rolled up in his blanket and immediately fell asleep. Hours later he awoke feeling fully rested and much stronger. He could tell it was early from the slight bit of grayish light showing at the cave entrance. He glanced up at the hole in the ceiling of the cavern and could see only darkness. Taking enough time to shave and put on a clean shirt, John finally took his Henry and left the cave. He carefully examined the approach to the cave as he walked down the incline, making sure he had left no evidence that he was using it as a hiding place.

Walking quickly, he worked his way down hill to the big cavern where the creek disappeared into the earth. The rushing sound made by the water entering the cavern grew to a roar as he approached. Several cottonwood trees, thick bushes, and lacy fern grew around and over the cave mouth. A mist rose from the water as it disappeared into the cave, indicating that it fell far enough to send up a spray. That mist kept the growth around the opening green and lush.

About ten feet from the left side of the cave opening John pushed the bushes aside and stepped through. He was standing less than six feet away from the stream. The sound of the water falling filled his head. No wonder the Indians had called the disappearing stream Death Water. The sound was uncanny.

Putting his right hand against the wall of the cave, he ignored the semi-darkness and walked confidently back into the hill about thirty feet. When he was beyond the reach of the mist the falling water created, he stopped. Searching around for a minute he finally struck a match and found a small kerosene lantern that had been hidden in a niche in the wall. He lit it and continued walking farther back into the cave.

This part of the cave turned away from the water. He could still hear the roar of the falls behind him, but the sound was much easier to bear. About a hundred feet away from the waterfall, he reached the area where Alec had been digging for gold. A pick and several other tools were leaning against a small sluice box. The box was rigged across a tiny stream that came from somewhere in the darkness at the back of the tunnel. Everything appeared to be exactly as Alec had left it.

"That sly old devil," John said to himself. He knew that if Alec had sold this section of his property to Blaine he surely had not told him there was any gold in this cavern, because if he had, someone would have investigated.

I'll bet he made up some story about keeping this hill to come back to someday. It would be just like him, even though he was headed for California. *Now, why do you suppose he was so careful to remind me of this place?*

John looked around the diggings for a few minutes, painstakingly checking the whole area where Alec had been working. He couldn't find anything unusual. He didn't know what he was looking for, or even if there was anything here for him to find. Maybe the old man just wanted to make sure he still knew how to find the mine in case he died. He finally gave up and left the cave the way he came. A few steps away he turned and stood still for a moment to look back at the entrance and make certain it was still well hidden.

John climbed back up past the cavern where he had hidden Prince and made his way through the rocks and small trees to reach a place where it was open enough for him to see the countryside. There was a thin wisp of smoke over the cook shack at Hostetter's place. It looked as though whoever had taken over the place was still there. He watched for a few minutes, but saw no one. Turning the

opposite direction, he looked over toward the valley and
Silver Creek Ranch. From his position, trees blocked the
view of the ranch buildings but he could see Blaine's herd
in the distance. Everything looked peaceful. It had been two
days since he had seen Andrea. He had one more day to
keep his promise to show up at the ranch.

Scanning Hostetter's place again, he caught a flicker of
movement to the east. Watching carefully he soon spotted
someone riding down the main road toward the ranch entrance. "I wonder where I've seen that little gray mustang
he's riding." John murmured as he watched the rider. The
man left the road and turned his horse into the scrubby oaks
that grew near the ranch gate. He continued riding toward
the house, but was carefully keeping out of sight of anyone
in the bunkhouse. From where he stood John could catch
occasional glimpses of the rider as he moved through the
trees.

Soon the rider came out behind the ranch house. He was
still well hidden from the windows of the bunkhouse by
the small orchard behind the house. He finally dismounted
and tied his horse to one of the trees. Walking between the
rows of trees and bending slightly to keep hidden, the man
approached the back of the bunkhouse.

John chuckled to see the man doing almost exactly what
he had done at the Double G a few nights before. "Hey,"
he said to himself, "I think that rider is Del Ketchum. I
want to talk to him."

Suddenly John realized that if he hurried he should be
able to reach the road where it curved around the foot of
the little mountain before Ketchum rode back that way.
Holding his rifle in front of him to keep from hitting it
against the trees, he all but ran down the hill. Breathing
hard, he finally reached the level and continued on through
the scrub oaks and mixed brush out to the edge of the main
road.

Leaning his Henry against a tree beside the dusty track,
John stepped out into the road and checked for tracks. Fresh
tracks led toward the Hostetter place, but the rider had

clearly not returned this way. John moved a short distance back into the brush to wait. It wasn't long before the rider came around a bend in the road. As he approached his hiding place, John recognized Del Ketchum.

John pushed his way through the brush and stepped out into the road. Ketchum was so surprised at his sudden appearance that he stopped his horse and yelled, "What are you doing, mister?" His hand dropped to his gun.

"You're Del Ketchum, aren't you?" John removed his hat so the man could get a clear view of his face.

"Well, I'll be. If it ain't Johnny Garrett. I thought you must be lying dead some place, you disappeared so completely." Ketchum dismounted and held out his hand to John.

"It's good to see you Del." John reached out to take the man's hand. He remembered Andrea saying Del had become a deputy sheriff and asked, "Where's your badge?"

"Go on now, I hid the dratted thing in my pocket." Ketchum looked sheepish as he retrieved the badge and pinned it back on the front of his shirt. "Don't you go holding that badge against me Johnny. I know it looks bad, but I can explain.

"Let's get out of the way a little here, so we can talk." Ketchum led his horse off the road and into the brush until he reached a group of oaks that would hide them from the road. John walked along behind him.

"Where's your horse?" Ketchum asked, looking at John quizzically.

"Oh, he's tied back in the woods a ways," John lied.

When they reached a shaded spot well back from the road, Ketchum tied his horse and sat down with his back against a tree. "Johnny, do you know what's going on around here? I mean, with your pa and Hostetter and the folks over to Silver Creek?"

John studied Ketchum's face. He had taken his hat off and put it on the ground beside him. He was probably thirty years old, but working outside in the sun had weathered him until he looked more like forty. His hair was mixed blonde and brown and his eyes were dark, either black or brown. The man had ridden for Hostetter for years. Surely he could trust him even if he was serving as a deputy sheriff.

"I'm not sure what's going on, Del. Will you tell me what you know about it?"

"How long have you been back around these parts, Johnny?" Ketchum looked wary.

John decided that he had best explain to Ketchum about his warning visit from the old man. "Alec Gunnison looked me up where I was working down in El Paso. He told me that my pa needed me. He said that Hostetter had been killed and that his outfit was broken up. I got the impression that Alec thought Pa or his foreman had taken over this property and run Hostetter's riders off. He told me that a herd of Double G cattle were grazing on the range. He wasn't sure if Pa was involved in shooting Hostetter or if Willis was, but he urged me to come home and find out what was going on. I ran in to one of Blaine's kids up north of the valley and that's how I learned that you were the only one of Hostetter's men still around and that you were serving as deputy to that sorry excuse for a sheriff."

"Sorry excuse for a sheriff. You can say that again. O'Riley is about the sorriest sheriff I ever saw. He belongs heart and soul to one man, that banker Hamilton." Ketchum's voice revealed a bitter contempt for both men.

"Hamilton." John shook his head in astonishment. "The Blaine kid thought the sheriff was a tool of my father's."

After thinking for a moment, he continued. "Look, Del, I'm going to tell you what I know. I need your help. I went in town two nights ago to see Asa Hamilton. I thought I could trust him to give me the straight story on what was going on with my father, but I didn't feel comfortable with him for some reason. He told me that Hostetter had been killed by rustlers, and Mrs. Hostetter had gone back East.

"My father had tried to buy the place two years ago, he said, and he had told him then that Mrs. Hostetter had left instructions not to sell the property to him. Hamilton claimed to be worried because my father hadn't been in town for two months. He had been sending Willis in with notes to get money for payroll.

"According to Hamilton, Willis came to the bank last week with a note from my father instructing him to sell the Hostetter place to Willis. The note said that Pa would stand good for payment. Hamilton said that Willis became threatening when he refused to handle such a deal with only a note to go on.

"I just listened. I never let on I knew anything, and when I left his office I told him I was going to see Ted Bennett before I left town. He let me out of his office and shut the door. As I was leaving town I heard a door shut and it sort of spooked me for some reason, so I hid. I watched for a little while and sure enough, someone was following me. Whoever it was passed me and continued out to the road on the edge of town. He stopped there for a minute, looking for me, then headed away from town at a run. It was too dark for me to tell who it was."

"That's easy enough to clear up," said Ketchum. "It was me that followed you."

"It was you." John jumped to his feet and stared down at Ketchum. "What the devil were you following me for?"

"Calm down, Johnny. Just calm down, please. I've been hanging around the bank and watching Hamilton. I saw you and him go in his office. I didn't know who you were, and I wanted to find out. I could tell easy enough you weren't Rafe Willis, or Sean O'Riley, but your horse looked familiar. It never crossed my mind it would be you, after six years. I realized right quick that no one was riding ahead of me on that road. I came back to town to try to find your horse. He wasn't anywhere on the street and I knew I couldn't track you in the dark, so I gave up."

"Why were you watching Hamilton?"

"I believe he's the key to this mystery. I'm convinced he had something to do with Hostetter's killing, I didn't have much to go on, but I've felt leery of him for years. I know now that he's involved with Willis, and both he and

Willis are involved with Sheriff O'Riley. I've seen Willis and O'Riley sneaking in Hamilton's office after banking hours several different times.

"When Hostetter was killed, I knew something about it smelled bad. I followed his cows tracks for miles and finally decided that they weren't really rustled. They were pushed over into that rough country back of your pa's place and scattered. I went to Miz Hostetter and told her what I had found, and when she left town she asked me to write to her if I could find out anything more. I hung around town and did pick-up jobs for almost a year after the outfit broke up. I wasn't having any luck finding out anything. So when I got the chance at the job of O'Riley's deputy I took it.

"I've been with O'Riley when he went out to the Double G a number of times. He always leaves me at the bunkhouse on some trumped up excuse and rides up to the house alone. I've noticed that Willis always lets him in the house. I haven't seen your pa the last three times we went out there, that's been almost two months now.

"I've also noticed that bunch of gun slicks Willis is hiring. No more than six riders out of your old crew are still there that I know of. There's an older guy named Neil and that kid you always rode with, I think his name is Jones. Jake Beale and his brother are still there. I don't remember the name of the other two, but I think they're brothers as well."

"I know Jake Beale and the others are good with their guns, but I can't believe they would side against my father. I know Neil Thompson and Bill Jones won't. Why do you suppose they've stayed on?" John asked.

"They might have the same reason I do. Hostetter was always good to me. He gave me work when I was down and out. And that ain't all. I know he did it at Mrs. Hostetter's encouragement. She deserves to have somebody try to find out who killed her man and make them pay for it." Ketchum frowned, and averted his face for a moment. Turning back to face John, he said, "Your pa is always good to his men too. I know he's hard, but even if he is they owe him."

John studied Ketchum's face. When he mentioned Mrs. Hostetter his eyes flashed and his expression became truly fierce. It occurred to John that it was possible the man had more reason than he was willing to say to try to find out what was happening and how it all tied in to Hostetter's killing.

"Del, do you realize that counting those six men still at the ranch, you and me, and the men at Blaine's ranch we might have enough men to stand up to that crew at the Double G if we had to?"

"Well, I don't know, Johnny. I ain't looking forward to no shooting war. We don't even know for sure who's a friend or who's an enemy yet. I've been over to the valley a couple of times and met with two of Blaine's riders that I've known for a few years. One of them is Burt Stillwell and the other guy that just goes by the name of Whitey. They think your pa sent men into the valley to kill one of Blaine's riders a couple of weeks ago."

"I'll never believe that, Del. I'm going to stay here and find out. Can I count on you to help me?"

"You bet you can. I think you're riding the same trail I am. If we untangle what's going on with Willis and Hamilton and your father, I figure we'll know who back-shot Tim Hostetter, or at least who ordered him killed."

"I'll come to town in a day or two. Can you sneak over to Ted Bennett's office and see if he'll tell you anything?"

"Heck, I've already tried that. He won't say anything about anything. Maybe he sees me riding as deputy for O'Riley and thinks I'm a crook too, I don't know." Ketchum looked uncomfortable. "I heard that Bennett is your good friend, John."

"He sure is, and I'll talk to him." John smiled. He and Ted Bennett had been the best of friends. They had shared a meal and spent time together every time John visited Hinton for years.

"When I know something I'll find you in town and say

I'll be heading out to the Double G. I'll leave town, but wait for you in that first patch of oaks near the main road. It's about three miles out."

"I'll be there." Ketchum reached out to shake John's hand. He led his horse back to the road and jumped into the saddle, still smiling, he waved his hand to John in a sort of salute.

Chapter Seven

The sun was low in the sky and most of the valley was in deep shadow when John rode out of the woods behind the buildings at Silver Creek. He rode boldly into the barnyard, waving his hand to the astonished man who had just stepped out of the cook shack.

"Hold it right there, fella!" the man yelled. He looked to be the cook. He was a little old for herding cows and had a towel tied around his waist. "Who in blazes are you and what do you mean by sneaking in here through them woods?"

"Don't get excited, cowboy, I'm harmless. My name is John Garrett. I'm here to see Mr. Blaine."

"I know for a fact Russ Blaine don't want to see no Garretts. He'll run you off with his shotgun."

"I sincerely hope not." Stepping down from the saddle, John was careful to keep his hands in the clear so the man could see them. He slowly unbuckled his gun belt and hung it over the saddle horn.

"I'm going to leave my horse here by the corral and walk around to the front of the house."

The man seemed to calm down a little as he watched John remove his gun and leave it on the saddle. He didn't say anything more, but caught John's eye and nodded. John could feel the man's eyes boring in his back as he walked

109

around the house. He mounted the front steps to cross the porch to the door. Russ Blaine jerked the door open before he could knock. John noticed that Blaine was big, probably equal to John's own height of two or three inches over six feet. His chest was like a barrel. A salt-and-pepper mustache matched his thick unruly looking hair. He looked furious. "You'll be Turner?" he demanded.

John removed his hat before he answered. He knew he had to choose his words carefully. Facing Blaine squarely he held his head up and looked him in the eye. "Your daughter knows me as Kyle Turner, Mr. Blaine, but that's not exactly my name."

Blaine continued to stare at him. He began to look less angry than puzzled. "Are you saying that you lied to my daughter about who you are?"

"Yes sir, I'm afraid I did. I really can explain, Mr. Blaine. I had a good reason."

"I can't see any reason for lying about who you are if you're honest, young fellow. What is your name?"

"I'm John Garrett, of the Double G."

"You're Garrett's son. Well, I'll be. I thought you and he had a falling out years ago and you left the country."

"That's essentially correct, sir, but an old friend told me there was trouble here, and my father was involved in it somehow. I felt I had to come home and at least try to find out what was happening. I didn't know who Andrea was at first, and I was wounded and helpless. I was afraid to tell her who I was."

"We've been thinking your father was behind our trouble for a long time, but things have gotten so bad lately we've come to believe we were mistaken. It's hard to accept that he would do some of the lowdown things that have happened."

"I hope my father hasn't taken to ordering men shot from ambush, sir, but I haven't found out much yet."

"Well, come in the house and we'll talk. I've been planning on going over to the Double G to talk to your father anyway."

Blaine turned and motioned for John to follow as he went in the house. He almost chuckled aloud when he thought of what his daughter's reaction would be when she learned that the man she had taken care of was Mason Garrett's son.

The main room of the ranch house was large and the last light of the day was shining in the windows across the front. A woman John assumed was Mrs. Blaine rose from a chair near the rock fireplace as the men entered. She kept her eyes on Blaine as she asked, "Should I fix some food for Mr. Garrett, Russ?"

"Yes, Julie. I'm sure you heard us talking. Let me introduce you to John Garrett of the Double G. Please fix him some supper. After he eats he's going to tell me a lot of things." Blaine gave John a meaningful look as he introduced him to his wife.

Following Blaine through the simple but beautiful room, John wondered where Andrea was. He almost asked Mrs. Blaine, but the rancher's eyes following his every movement made him decide to wait for a better time.

"I appreciate your hospitality, Mrs. Blaine." He smiled at the woman as she indicated a chair beside the large round table in the kitchen. "A home-cooked meal is always a treat."

"Thank you, Mr. Garrett. I really enjoy cooking and I like it when hungry men appreciate my work." She quickly placed a heaping plate of food before him and positioned a platter of homemade light bread beside it. Then she poured a cup of coffee for each of the men. Blaine thanked his wife and nodded, then she returned to the front room. She apparently understood some signal Blaine had made that he wanted to talk to his visitor alone.

The rancher watched as John ate the delicious beef and vegetables Mrs. Blaine had given him. When he finished eating, John took up his coffee cup and without waiting for Blaine to ask questions he began to tell his story.

"Your information that my father and I had a falling out is right, Mr. Blaine. We differed on how to handle something and had an argument. I'm afraid our tempers got so far out of hand that he offered to take his bull whip to me, and I swore that I'd shoot him if he did. He ordered me off the ranch and I left.

"I think he probably thought I would just stay away a few days and then come on back home after I cooled off, but I had to face the truth. Pa just couldn't stand for me to be truly in charge of the ranch. He had made me foreman two years before, and I tried my best, but he just wouldn't turn loose. He was always countermanding my orders to the men, and he refused to let me make any changes in the way we handled things. If it did nothing else, our fight made it plain to me that we'd both be better off if I tried my luck somewhere else.

"Alec Gunnison was friends with two brothers named Wilson who had a ranch near El Paso. From what he had told me about the two men I figured I might like to know them, so I worked my way down there. It took me a while, because I left the ranch with only a little money and I was too mad and too proud to stop in Hinton and charge the supplies I needed for traveling to my father's account.

"I had been with the Wilsons nearly three years and had worked my way up to Segundo. One evening last month I was going to the bunkhouse and there was Alec standing on the porch. He told me he had sold out to you and was on his way to California. He said he had looked me up because there was some sort of trouble here that involved my father. He told me it was my duty to go home and help him. He either couldn't or wouldn't tell me any more than that. I didn't want to agree that I had a duty to help my father if he needed me, but after I slept on it that night I knew I had to come back and try, whether my father wanted me or not.

"I got in a fracas across the river on the way here and got shot. I stayed on my horse until I reached the big pines at the north end of your place and then I just gave out. I guess I fainted and fell off my horse. Your daughter found me lying in the a grassy spot in the big pines, bleeding. I was so addled from losing blood and hurting that when she said her name was Andy I thought she was a boy.

"Your daughter is a brave young woman, Mr. Blaine," John said. "You can certainly be proud of her. She never hesitated to help me when she saw I was wounded. She saved my life."

Blaine didn't say anything for what seemed like forever to John. He finally held out his hand. "I'm going to ask your forgiveness for not shaking your hand before, son. I'm glad to meet you. I understand why you were careful and so will Andrea."

"I'm glad to meet you, sir." John smiled as he shook Blaine's hand. "Now where is Andrea hiding?"

Blaine laughed aloud. He got up and crossed the kitchen to a door on John's left. He tapped on the panels and called out, "Come on out girl. I know you've heard everything that's been said."

The door opened instantly. Andrea was dressed in a white blouse and a divided riding skirt. Her gleaming hair was brushed smooth. There was no trace left of the boyish "Andy."

John pushed his chair back and stood up. *She's beautiful*, he thought. He had trouble finding his voice. "Miss Blaine—Andrea. I'm here. Just as I promised you I would be."

Andrea stopped a moment when she reached the other side of the table from John and studied his face. She could see that he was astounded at her transformation. She hoped the change had the effect she wanted. Finally she spoke. "Mr. Garrett. I'll have to learn to call you that now."

"I know. My name is John Kyle Garrett. I'm sure you're angry with me if you heard everything I said to your father. Can you forgive me?"

"I understand why you lied to me when I found you. You didn't know me at first, but why didn't you tell me the truth after you knew I wouldn't bring any harm to you?"

Her eyes bored into his. John dropped his head. "I don't

know. I knew you would find out soon enough. I guess I was trying to gain as much time as I could so I would be strong enough to handle trouble if it came."

"In other words, you didn't trust me."

"That's not true. You saved my life and I did trust you. I—I can't explain any better." John waited for her answer.

Andrea turned from the table and taking a cup from a cupboard, she filled it with coffee and took a seat at the table. "I forgive you, Mr. Garrett," she said coolly. "Please sit down. I think I'm entitled to be in on this discussion."

John returned to his seat. He felt confused and almost angry. Andrea's seemed far away and so different as to be another person. It wasn't just the change in her clothes, either. Where was the kind and companionable little person he had gotten to know in the cabin? He watched her stir sugar in her coffee as she studiedly ignored him.

The outside door to the kitchen opened suddenly and a young man John took to be Bill Blaine rushed in. "Hey Dad, there's a strange sorrel horse out—" He stopped speaking suddenly to stare at John.

"Shut the door, Billy," Blaine said, "and come on in. You need to meet this fellow. Shake hands with John Garrett."

The younger Blaine looked puzzled and then angry. "You've got a nerve, Garrett. Sitting right here in our house, after what your people have done to us."

"Hold it, Blaine." John stepped around the table and held out his hand. "I haven't been involved in anything at the Double G for almost six years. I have no quarrel with you or anyone else around here. I came here to try to find the source of the troubles and to try and stop it."

Russ Blaine yelled at his son, "When I introduce you to a man in our home I expect you to keep a civil tongue in your head, young man. Now, you take this man's hand."

Bill Blaine shook John's hand quickly, refusing to look at him. He took a chair at the table beside his father without further speech and glared at John.

John looked across the table at the three Blaines. They

were handsome people. The old man must have been something when he was young. He was still big and strong and fine looking. Andrea was so beautiful she would probably break the heart of every cowboy in the county. The brother looked and acted younger than Andrea, but he remembered her telling him that he was older.

Andrea interrupted his observations to ask, "Have you found out anything about who's behind the attacks on our men and the raids on our cattle?"

"Andrea, Mr. Blaine, based on what I know of my father I honestly don't think it's him. I'm suspicious of some people, but I have no proof. I plan to go to Hinton and find out what Ted Bennett can tell me. I believe the roots of this trouble lie in the Hostetter property. I understand that Bennett either has control of that place himself or may know who has. He also may have learned something about Hostetter's shooting from Elaine Hostetter before she left the area."

"Why do you think your father isn't mixed up in things?" Bill Blaine asked in a demanding voice. "He's the one that's been trying so hard to buy us out. The last offer he made was so high it was crazy."

"Hmm . . . just how high was that offer?" John asked.

Russ Blaine answered. "The offer was for almost twice what I paid for the place. But remember Billy, we're not for sure that Garrett actually made that last offer. It was delivered to me in a very unpleasant way by Rafe Willis, Garrett's foreman."

"What's that got to do with anything? Willis couldn't make such an offer without Garrett backing him up, could he?" Billy asked.

"I think that crazy offer Willis made goes a long way to explain this trouble. I've talked to a dozen people who have known Mason Garrett for years. They agree with me that he'd push like the devil to get what he wants, but they insist that he's just not the type to bushwhack a man. I've only known him for about five years, but I have to agree with them. Some sorry somebody shooting down one of my riders from ambush completely changes everything. I wanted to believe my enemy was Garrett, it seemed to make everything simpler, but I know someone else has to be behind this."

John Garrett smiled in relief. "Thank you, Mr. Blaine. You'll never know how much I appreciate you saying that. I don't believe my father is capable of bushwhacking a man and I don't believe he would stand for anyone who worked for him doing it. There's something more going on than we understand, and I'm determined to find out what it is.

"I made a trip to the Double G a few nights ago. I couldn't get close enough to the house to find out anything, but there are too many men in the bunkhouse, and they don't act like cowboys. I'm beginning to think my father may be dead, and Willis has taken over and is acting on his own."

"What can we do to help?" Andrea asked, looking concerned.

"Just what you've been doing, Andrea. Stay here and be ready to protect your ranch if necessary."

"I just plain hate sitting here and waiting for trouble to come to me," Blaine said, shaking his head.

John chuckled. "I'll bet you do. It's the best way, though. This valley can be defended. How many men do you have?

"Don't tell him that, Dad," Billy said. "How can you be sure he ain't just spying for his father or that Willis?"

"Billy," Andrea burst out. Her expression was a mixture of anger and embarrassment. "How can you say that? Haven't you been listening to anything Daddy or Mr. Garrett said?"

"You be quiet, Bill," Blaine said firmly. "I came to the understanding in my own mind days ago that Garrett couldn't be shooting my men and stealing my stock. What this man says rings true, and I mean to work with him. That means you'll have to do the same son, whether you like it or not."

"Well, I don't like it." Bill rose from the table. "I'm

going to the bunkhouse. I think you've lost your mind."
He pushed his chair back and left the house.

It was gray and misty in the forest just before dawn. The
sun had barely begun to color the sky when John turned
Prince onto the road to Hinton. He urged the horse to a
trot, holding his rifle across his lap and keeping a close
watch. He knew that there would be no way he could avoid
being seen if anyone who knew him happened to be riding
along the road. Asa Hamilton had probably already told
some people he was back. If the banker had secret meetings
with Rafe Willis like Del Ketchum said, he certainly would
have told him. He had probably told Sheriff O'Riley as
well.

John knew he had to give up on his idea to keep hidden
until he found out what was going on. It didn't really matter
anymore. He had to talk to Ted Bennett. The lawyer should
be able to help him understand who was behind the attacks
on Blaine's men, and what was going on with his father.
He probably could tell him something more about the Hostetter shooting as well.

It had occurred to him again as he was talking to Blaine
the night before that his father might be dead. That would
explain a lot. If Mason Garrett were dead, Rafe Willis
would have access to all of his papers. That would make
it a simple matter for him to forge his father's hand on the
notes he brought to the banker. He could just keep on asking for funds to make payroll and buy supplies until he was
ready to make his move. If Willis and the banker were
working together somehow, that trick could work forever.
There was one thing about it that was a puzzle to John.
Why had Hamilton gone out of his way to tell him about
refusing to act on a note from his father ordering him to
sell the Hostetter property to Willis?

The sun was bright when John stopped under the oaks
at Red Spring to spell his horse and rest a few minutes. He
was no more than ten minutes from town. If he rode in by
way of the alley behind the hotel, he should be able to get

to Bennett's place without running into too many people
who knew him. He didn't want to have to explain himself
to the whole town.

Bennett lived in quarters in the same building that held
his office, so when John got no answer at his office door
he walked up the stairs and knocked on the door of his
rooms. Bennett took his time coming to the door.

When John knocked the second time he heard Bennett
call out impatiently, "I'm coming, for goodness sakes."

He blinked in astonishment when he saw John standing
just outside the door. "Am I still asleep or am I seeing
things? I had begun to think you were never coming back
home." Grinning, he reached to shake John's hand. "I'm
glad to see you, Johnny, come on in and have some food
with me."

John suddenly realized he was glad to see Ted. They had
become friends in the years since the lawyer had begun
taking care of ranch business for his father. They had spent
some time together when John served as his father's foreman and Bennett took care of some of the legal matters
that were inevitable in running a ranch.

"I'm here, Ted, and I can hardly believe I'm saying it,
but I'm glad to see you, you old swindler."

Laughing, John stepped inside the lawyer's sitting room.
Nothing had changed. Entering in this room had always
been like stepping into a picture. The room was furnished
with dark antique furniture. If the elegant furniture weren't
unusual enough this far away from civilization, a magnifi-
cent oriental carpet covered the entire floor, its muted col-
ors gleaming in the sunlight that shone in the windows. A
large, comfortable-looking chair was near the fireplace with
a reading lamp on a small table beside it. Nearby was a
glass-fronted bookcase filled with books.

Ted had ridden into Hinton with a group of ragged-
looking miners more than twelve years earlier. The miners
continued on west, but Ted stayed in town. He had looked
just like the rest of the men in his party when he arrived.
He was bearded, his hair was long and he was dressed in

rough clothing. He refused a bed in the common room of the hotel, though. He demanded a room to himself and ordered a hot bath.

A few hours later, a tall, handsome, and distinguished looking gentleman with smooth, pale hair came to the hotel desk and asked where he could find a decent meal. The hotel clerk could only recognize him as the rough miner who had rented the room by his piercing blue eyes. Ted was clean-shaven and dressed in a suit that had been tailored to fit his tall frame.

He nosed around Hinton for the next few days and finally bought the best building in town. He paid for it with cash money. After hanging out his shingle as an attorney, he locked up his new office and left town without even waiting for his first client to turn up. It was September when Bennett left Hinton headed east and riding horseback. He pulled back into town late the next June with his furniture, books, and other treasures loaded on two huge wagons.

Ted liked his comforts. He took particularly good care of himself and his possessions. John had enjoyed spending time with him. He admired the way the man managed to get pleasure from everything from food to good books to just sitting around and talking. He was a wicked card player, but he only played with friends and never for money. He didn't seem to need or want money.

"Come on in the dining room, John," Ted said. "Rosa always cooks enough for three people, just grab yourself a plate from the sideboard over there and dig in."

Ted placed a napkin and a knife and fork on the table across from his plate. Sliding a plate of ham and potatoes closer so John could reach the serving spoon, he poured another cup of coffee. "Here, have a couple of these soda biscuits. I had a hard time teaching a great Mexican cook to make these, but she finally learned. They're as good as you'll find anywhere."

Ted chattered about various people that he knew John would be interested in while they ate breakfast. When there were no more biscuits or other food left, he poured them both another cup of coffee and leaned back in his chair and grinned as he said. "I see that Alec Gunnison found you."

"What do you mean, Ted?" John was surprised. "What do you know about Alec finding me?"

"He and I talked about your father needing you. He didn't say it, but I figured that was the reason he left here. He told around that he was on the way to California, but he was looking for you."

"When he left me in El Paso he told me he was on the way to California." Seeing the negative to that in Ted's eyes, John cursed. "That slick old buzzard. He lied to me. Where in the world is he now?"

"Would you believe he's holed up in Hostetter's old bunkhouse with a couple of old ranger friend of his from down in Texas?"

"Well, if that don't beat all. I guess I'll have to believe it. I heard that someone's been forted up at in that bunkhouse for weeks. The fella that told me about it thought it was some of the new riders from the Double G because Hostetter's range is full of Double G cattle." John's expression was a combination of disgust and astonishment. He was growing angry as he thought of Alec tricking him into leaving a good job, making that long trip and getting shot in the process.

"Don't get your back up, my friend," Ted continued. "Alec put those men there several weeks ago. He'd been forced to drive Willis and some of his gunslinger riders off with a rifle two different times. He knew he couldn't handle much more by himself, so he came into town and telegraphed for those friends of his. He left them to guard the ranch so he could go find you. He was so excited when he left I believed he already knew where you were. I think one of those friends of his may have told him when he answered Alec's telegraph."

"Why in heck couldn't he have explained things to me, didn't he trust me?" John's voice rose with indignation.

"Of course he trusts you. You know he has always hoped you and your father would make up your quarrel. I guess he thought if he could convince you that it was your duty to help your father, that would do the trick."

"Tell me what's going on with my father."

"I'm afraid I can't tell you that. Your father hasn't been to see me for in a while. I don't know what to think. He and I had a sort of falling out about two years ago. He wanted to buy the Hostetter place and he got plenty irritated with me because I said it wasn't for sale. He claimed it was for sale, but for some reason Elaine Hostetter had left orders with Hamilton over at the bank that it couldn't be sold to him. He demanded that I give him her address in Boston, and when I wouldn't he refused to even speak to me for several months.

"He finally needed some papers I had in my safe, and came in my office as if nothing had happened. I told Alec the old man would probably do the same thing with you. If you had come on back home six years ago and just gone on about your business as if nothing was different, he would have pretended nothing had ever happened between you two."

Lowering his coffee cup John said sternly, "Stop dancing around things, Ted. I want to know what's going on."

"Okay . . . okay. I'll tell you. I guess I've talked around things until I'm in the habit. Let's go back about two years. Tim Hostetter and his wife were my clients. He told me he had lost cattle and that he was watching his herd, trying to catch the man who was stealing them. I'm sure you remember that he didn't have a lot of cows, but the ones he had weren't just ordinary old Spanish cattle. They were crossbred with some heavier breed of cattle. He was planning on building up a herd and waiting for the railroad to come closer before he tried to market any.

"The last time he was here he told me he thought his cows were being taken by one man, because whoever it was never took over four or five cows at a time. The rustler always waited for a good rain and drove the cattle through the pines and into the rocks over near Milton's gulch. Even if Hostetter could follow their trail to the rocks, he would lose it there. He had searched the area, but the trail just vanished."

Rosa, Bennett's Mexican housekeeper, came into the room. Ted rose from his chair. "Let's go around to my office so Rosa can clean this table. I'll want to show you some papers later anyway."

John followed him through the sitting room and down the staircase. Bennett unlocked the door to his office and motioned for John to enter, shutting and locking the door after they entered. "We might as well have some privacy," he said. "I don't expect anyone, but there's a lot of people interested in my business nowadays, I don't think I'll take a chance."

As soon as they were seated in the office, Ted continued talking. "Elaine Hostetter came in here late one afternoon and said she had found her husband out near their herd, shot to death. He had left the house late the night before, telling her he was going to "trap" the rustlers. She was concerned and urged him not to go, but he assured her he would be all right and left. She waited up for hours, hoping he would come back. It got really late, so she finally went to bed. When she woke up the next morning and realized he hadn't come home, she had a horse saddled and took two of their riders with her out on the range to look for him.

"They found Hostetter's body lying on the ground right out in the open. His horse was standing near him. It had been raining, of course, and there were no tracks except the ones his horse had made just moving around nibbling on grass. She took his body home and with the help of her housekeeper and maid, laid him out in her parlor. Then she rode in here herself to get me and the sheriff.

"It happened that the sheriff was out of town, so she came straight over to my office. I went with her to make arrangements with our doctor who also serves as Hinton's undertaker to ride out there and do what needed to be done, then I rode on out to her place with her.

"When we got to the ranch, Alec Gunnison was sitting

on the front porch. I found out later that Elaine had sent a rider to get him before she started for town. Alec had been away from the cabin hunting when the rider got over there so it was a couple of hours before he got home. He had ridden in just ahead of us. Elaine invited us both in the house and led the way down the hall to her husband's office. When we got in the room, she shut the door and went over to sit behind the desk. Then she announced that she was selling the ranch to Alec and going back home to Boston.

"Before I got over that, she surprised me again by turning to Alec and sort of announcing, 'Alec, I know you want this place for Johnny Garrett, so I'm going to sell it to you today if you still want it, on one condition. I want you to keep the sale a secret.' I knew she wanted me to handle the sale, and I said, 'Elaine, the minute we file a deed at the courthouse the sale will no longer be a secret.'

"She said I didn't have to file the deed. That she would sign two copies. Alec would send you a copy and she would put the other one in the safe there in the office until the men who killed her husband were apprehended and it was safe to make the sale public. I asked her then why she felt keeping the deed transfer secret would help find her husband's killer. She said she was sure it was your father who ordered her husband's murder, and she believed he would kill anyone else who got in his way, so she didn't want to put Alec at risk.

"I tried to reason with her, but she wouldn't hear anything but that your father was the only one who was after her ranch, that he had tried several times to buy it and was angry because they wouldn't sell to him. She blamed him for rustling their cattle and for killing her husband. She swore that's what she was going to tell the sheriff before she left for the east.

"I sat down at Tim's desk and drew up the papers transferring the property. Elaine called her housekeeper and foreman in to witness her signature. She and Alec had obviously already made a deal for the property, because she had me draw the deed to say he was paying her 'ten dollars and other good and valuable considerations.' I have no idea what their deal was.

"It wasn't three days later she came in the office the second time and made me swear once again to keep the deal on the ranch a secret. She signed instructions for me to have her money transferred to a bank back east and left town with her housekeeper and maid in that big coach of hers. Her foreman and Del Ketchum were acting as outriders. I guess she went all the way up to Flagstaff to catch a train, because Ketchum and the other man came back through town a few days later driving the coach.

"Your father did want her ranch, she was right about that. When I told him it was sold and wouldn't tell him what the buyer's name was I thought sure he would hit me. I will not believe he killed Hostetter, though John. I've known him too long to believe he'd order a killing to get what he wants."

John had been pacing the floor of the office as the lawyer was talking. He ran his hand through his hair as he turned to face Bennett. "I just can't figure anything, Ted. The more I learn about this, the more confused I feel."

John returned to his chair and leaning his forearms on the desk he asked, "Do you know what Asa Hamilton has to do with all this?"

"Asa Hamilton wants the land. He tried to buy it from Elaine Hostetter when she went into the bank to get some cash for her trip. I was there. I heard her tell him he couldn't buy the property and to tell your father he couldn't buy it either. I don't know what she knew, or what she thought she knew, but it seemed as though she was trying to stir something up with the banker and your father."

"Tell me how Sean O'Riley and Rafe Willis fit into this puzzle," John asked.

"I can't tell you that, my friend, because I have no idea. Both of them have been in here several times and tried to get me to talk about Elaine Hostetter's business. In fact, they came in here together last week and said they wanted to get up a posse and drive the 'squatters' off the Hostetter ranch. Well, I couldn't tell them Alec had bought the ranch so I told them I'd have to write to Mrs. Hostetter before they could do anything, because she might have sent someone out there without telling me. I'm not sure they really believed that, but they finally gave up and left.

"The only person who really knows the whole story is Alec Gunnison. As far as I know he's out at the Hostetter ranch. He came in town a few days ago and told me if anyone came asking for him I should tell them to ride out to the ranch with a flag of truce. He wouldn't tell me who it was he was expecting, but I should have figured out that it had to be you."

John got up and grabbed his hat. "I'm heading out there, then. I'll see Alec, then I'll come back to town in a couple of days. There has to be some sense in all of this somewhere. I hope he can explain."

"Wait a minute, John. Don't be in such a hurry." Bennett stood up to come around the desk.

"Ted, I think my father may be dead, from the way Willis has been acting. I have to find out. I'll be back." John turned and left the lawyer's office.

Chapter Eight

As he left Bennett's office and started toward his horse to leave town, John suddenly remembered his promise to see Del Ketchum. He tied his sorrel behind the hotel and he walked through the alley and up the street to the sheriff's office. The office was empty. He crossed the street to the saloon. Sheriff O'Riley and Del Ketchum were sitting at a table in the center of the room playing cards with two men John didn't recognize. A bottle of whiskey sat in the center of the table.

Lowering his head so his hat brim obscured his face, John went up to the bar and ordered a beer. He dropped a coin on the bar, picked up the glass, and walked over to sit at a table in the back corner of the saloon. The sheriff and the two men with him seemed to be examining him as he glanced their way, but Ketchum ignored him.

After about five minutes, Ketchum rose from his chair and stretched. "I'm quitting this game," he said. "We just trade coins back and forth. Nobody ever wins or loses. Takes all the fun out of poker."

"Oh, shut up and play, Del," the sheriff said. "It ain't the same to play poker three-handed."

"Nah, I'm tired, I didn't get much sleep last night. I'm going to the office. Maybe I can get a little sleep over there."

"Well go on then, you polecat, if that's what you want," Sheriff O'Riley said. He picked up the whiskey bottle and poured drinks for him self and the other two men. "We can play poker without the likes of you."

Ketchum pushed open the double doors and left the saloon without looking back. John stayed where he was long enough to finish his beer, then he walked out of the saloon and turned down the street in the opposite direction of the sheriff's office. When he got to the end of the saloon, he ran through the alley to the back of the building and turned toward the sheriff's office.

Del was standing in the back door of the jail when John arrived. He motioned for John to stand well back as though they didn't know each other and said in a low voice, "I can meet you at that row of cottonwoods three miles east of town about dark. Turn off into the woods on the left."

He began to talk in a loud voice. "You head west and north of town, mister, take the second turn off. It's only about five miles out. There's an old sign post there where you turn, you can't miss it."

John nodded and replied in a clear voice, trying to make sure anyone listening to the conversation would assume he was a stranger. "I sure do thank you, deputy." He touched the front of his hat brim. "Good day."

He turned away from Del to walk back to the main street. As he moved along the sidewalk John saw several people he knew, but he kept his hat brim down over his face as much as possible and they didn't notice him. *I guess they don't expect to see me, so I'm as good as invisible,*" he thought, shaking his head.

When he reached Prince, John mounted and walked the horse to the western edge of town as though he was following the deputy's directions. As soon as he was far enough down the road so no one from town could see him, he turned north into the woods and circled back to the road leading west.

When he reached the line of cottonwoods Del had described, John turned off into the scrubby trees. Keeping close to the creek, he walked his horse about two hundred yards from the road until he came to an opening in the trees with a small patch of good grass. Dismounting, he took the bit out of Prince's mouth so he could graze. He pulled his rifle from the saddle and sat down to rest his shoulders against the bole of a large tree and wait for Del, holding the Henry across his lap.

John soon began to doze. He had missed hours of sleep the last few nights. He shook his head periodically to try to keep awake, but he soon fell into a sound asleep. Awakening with a start, he reached for his rifle. Prince was across the little clearing, peacefully grazing. He couldn't see or hear anything amiss. Rubbing the sleep out of his eyes he straightened his shoulders, but continued to rest against the tree. It was almost dark. It wasn't long before he heard a rustling in the bushes between his position and the road. He stood up to wait with his rifle ready, just in case. A minute or two later Del stepped out of the brush leading his horse.

"I stopped long enough to wipe out any tracks we left coming off the road. I could have tracked you back in here with one eye closed," Del said as he loosened his horses bridle and dropped the reins so he could graze.

Del walked over to John with his hand out. They shook hands and sat down near the big tree. Del seemed to study John's face for a few seconds then he dropped a bombshell. "John, I saw your father yesterday."

"You actually saw him!" John cried out in astonishment. "I had made sure he was dead. I couldn't make anything fit otherwise." He jumped up and paced back and forth in agitation.

"Take it easy. Take it easy." Ketchum held up his hand. "You were almost right about that, I think. There's definitely something wrong with him. I only caught a glimpse of him from a distance and through a window. He was sitting in one of those big chairs that fold back almost like a bed. I didn't see him move, either.

"I honestly think I was meant to see him," Ketchum continued. "O'Riley had me go with him out to the ranch. When we rode up, he motioned for me to come with him up to the house. Every other time I've been out there with him he's ordered me to go to the bunkhouse and wait for him. This time he had me wait by the hitching rail at the front of the house."

"What do you think it means?" John asked.

"I'll be darned if I know." Ketchum shook his head. "But I know how you may be able to find out. Did you notice those two fellas with O'Riley?"

"Sure I did," John answered. "I didn't recognize them when I was in the saloon, but I've been thinking about it and I think the big one was Winston Slade. He's a known gunfighter out of Wichita, Kansas."

"Well, I just happened to come back from breakfast a little early this morning and heard them talking as I came in the back door of the office. Willis sent those two men into town to watch for you or Alex Gunnison. Part of their job is to make sure neither of you make it out to the Double G. I almost laughed out loud when neither one of them recognized you in the saloon.

"According to what I heard, those men are also supposed to get rid of Neil Thompson and four more of your old riders who are still working on your pa's place. Willis has ordered them to move out to the line shack nearest town. They've been told to ride herd on a big bunch of cows and fifty or sixty horses that Willis is moving up there so they'll be near the water.

"I heard them saying that Willis gave orders for Slade and that Jackson kid that's his sidekick to sneak up on that line shack and kill the men staying there. He's to lose their bodies and gear. I suppose if anybody asks about them Willis will claim they just got a wild hair and decided to take off for parts unknown."

"That low-down snake." John snarled. "Were Slade and Jackson still in town when you left?"

"Yes they were, but they could wait until dark and if they cut across country they'd get out there in only about an hour. We're supposed to have a bright moon later to-night. They'll have no trouble traveling."

"Del, we have to get to the line shack before they do. Those men worked for me, I have to warn them. Two men won't be able to take that bunch if I warn them what's supposed to happen."

"I don't know about 'we' getting there—those men might shoot me on sight. I know they'll think I'm a spy for O'Riley and Willis."

"You're probably right about that. Why don't you stay in town and keep on watching Hamilton's office. Willis might decide it would be good for him to visit Hamilton tonight to create a good alibi in case he ever needed it. I'll ride straight on out there to the line shack."

"You be careful, John. Those men are probably pretty skittish. Make sure they know who you are before you give them a clear shot at you."

John chuckled. "I'll be careful. But hold on a minute. I have to tell you some things before I go, Del. I found out this morning that Alec Gunnison bought Hostetter's place. The 'squatters' holed up in the bunkhouse are Alec and some of his friends. As soon as I let Neil Thompson and the other Double G riders know what's going on I'm head-ing that way."

"Alec Gunnison bought the place? Well, heck. I thought Miz Hostetter just refused to sell the place to anybody." Ketchum looked puzzled, then his face flushed as though he were angry.

"Did you ever hear Mrs. Hostetter or her husband say anything about Hamilton?" John asked. "He told me that what Mrs. Hostetter told him was that he was not to sell the ranch to my father. He seemed to have the idea that she was willing to sell to anyone else. According to Ham-ilton, she sort of gave him the impression that she expected him to handle the sale."

Both men fell silent. John had a lot to think about. *What could be going on with his father? What was going on with Alec?*

Del was the first to speak. "We're not going to figure this out sitting here talking, Johnny. If you're going to be any help to those riders of yours you're going to have to ride. I'll git on back to town and watch Hamilton's office. I might be able to git close enough to the back window of the bank to hear something important if he has another late visitor."

"You're right." John caught up Prince's reins and settled the bit back in his mouth. Returning his rifle to its place on the saddle he mounted and turned to Del. "Come out to Hostetter's ranch late tomorrow evening if you can. I'll watch for you if I'm there. If not, the signal I've been given is a flag of truce. You use it too when you get there. I'll tell them you're coming."

"I'll be there. You get moving. You can't let those killers sneak up on those men. Besides, we're going to need their help."

John could hear Del and his horse crashing against branches as he worked his way through the brush back to the road. He walked Prince across the creek and turned south. The night was still dark, but he was in the open and he let Prince pick his way at a fast walk.

He was nearing patches of scrub oaks when the moon began to light up the sky. As the light increased he could see well enough to push the horse to a faster gait. Following a vague path between the groups of trees, it wasn't long before he came out on Garrett range near the line shack. John dismounted and holding his hand on Prince's nose to make sure he didn't neigh when he smelled other horses, he walked quietly toward the cabin, keeping close to the trees.

"Stop right there, you sneak." The voice came from the trees.

John was only about a hundred yards away from the cabin. He stopped and raised his hands high. Praying the man was one of the Double G cowboys, John said, "I'm a friend."

"Yeah, and I'm a Chinaman. Start walking toward the

shack." A tall, thin man stepped out of the shadow of the trees. He was holding a rifle. He motioned with the rifle for John to move ahead of him.

Dropping Prince's reins, John obeyed. "Hey, Thompson, do you have a match on you?"

"Shut up. I don't know how you know my name, but you can talk in a few minutes. After we get to the shack."

The rider whistled as they approached the shack. The door opened and another man called out. "Can I strike a light?"

"Yeah, I think this fella's alone. I only heard one horse."

"Come on in, I'll get the lantern."

John chuckled as he recognized the second man's voice. As he stepped into the doorway of the cabin he asked. "How are you, Jake?"

"Wait a minute," the man with the rifle in John's back said. "Johnny Garrett? You're Johnny Garrett?"

As the light from the lantern filled the room the five men crowded around John, patting him on the back, shaking his hand, and all talking at once.

Finally getting an opening to be heard in the hubbub, John said, "Now that you all know who I am, please douse that light. I came to warn you that two gun slicks are on their way out here from Hinton to wipe you boys out. It would sure make it easy if they rode up about now."

Blowing out the lantern he was holding, Jake Beale said, "We knew there was something fishy when Willis sent us all out here together. The job needed about two men, not five experienced riders. That's why Neil was on lookout. We had a feeling something might happen."

"I should have known you'd be on guard, but Del Ketchum warned me that Slade and that kid sidekick of his were supposed to come out here and kill you men and hide your bodies and your gear. I figured I'd try to beat him here. Willis was going to put out the story that you all had suddenly decided to grab a few Double G cows to turn into cash and leave the country."

"How in the world did Del Ketchum find that out?" Neil

asked. In the dim moonlight John couldn't really read facial expressions, but the man sounded suspicious. "More than that, why would he warn us?"

"Del's working for O'Riley so he can find out who killed Tim Hostetter. I think he's kind of sweet on Elaine Hostetter and he may have promised her he would find whoever killed her husband and see he was punished. He was back in the jail part of the sheriff's office this morning and overheard Sheriff O'Riley talking to Slade and the kid about the job."

The men crowded around John. Jake Beale asked, "What do you think we should do, boss?"

John smiled at the loyalty of the men. They had been his top riders and he should have known they would stick. "I have a perfect place for you men to hole up and I need your help. I'll explain what I plan to do as soon as we're out of here and safe. Will you ride with me?"

One by one the men stated their willingness to help. Neil Thompson seemed to be their spokesman. "Johnny, we've been so bamboozled for more than a year, we couldn't figure nothing. That Rafe Willis has run off all the newer riders and done everything he could to get us to leave of our own accord. We've had to do all the dirty work on the ranch. We stuck because we owe your old man. He's a cantankerous old catamount, but he's been more than fair to us."

"Let's get out of this trap, boys. You can tell me what all's been going on at the ranch later." John headed for the door to the cabin. The men grabbed up their bedrolls and followed.

"Lead your horse, Johnny," Neil Thompson whispered. "Our horses are still saddled and tied back here in the thicket. We figured we might need them sudden like, so we hid them."

Suddenly, Jake Beale made a sound like he'd been hit in the stomach and stumbled against Thompson. John heard the boom of a rifle behind them. He grabbed Jake's arm and helped drag him along with the men as they ran to the comparative safety of the woods.

"That son-of-a-gun shot me," Jake complained. "I'm all right, fellas. He only singed my ribs. Go kill the sorry back-shooter."

Holding their rifles ready, the men began to spread out in the wooded area. "Stay close enough to know who you're shooting at, men." John warned. He turned his rifle on a suspicious looking shadow near the cabin. His shot brought an answering muzzle flash. His shot had been several feet too high. Steadying his gun on a half-rotten stump John knelt to aim lower and fired again. This time he heard a strange thump and a strangling sound. He had hit one of them.

Neil touched John on his shoulder and whispered, "I'm going to work my way down past the cabin and try to get behind them. I think you got that one, but there's no way to be sure yet. I'd like to know both of them are hit at least, before we try to move on them."

"Go ahead," John answered. "We'll keep them busy."

The men kept up a withering fire toward the cabin. After a few minutes John crawled over to the men. "Ease up boys, I hear something."

When the firing stopped, they could plainly hear the hoof beats of a running horse off to the east.

Bill Jones jumped up and ran into the woods. It wasn't long before they could hear the pounding hooves of another horse running in the same direction.

"Bill will catch the murdering son of a gun. His dun is the runningest pony on this range," Jake said.

"Come on, Johnny, let's find out if that owlhoot you shot is alive. We might even get some information out of him."

Guns ready, John and the men walked slowly toward the cabin. The moon glinted off a rifle lying near the step. "I think it's safe to strike a light," Jake said.

The flare of the match revealed the bloody face of the gunman. He had a hole just below his left eye. It was Slade. John recognized the man from the bar. He was the older of the men he had seen sitting in the saloon with the sheriff. "So it was the kid that took off. We got lucky. Slade wouldn't have given up so quickly."

"You're right about that. We owe you something for getting here when you did, Johnny. We were kind of expecting something to happen, but we might not have gotten by so easy if you hadn't been here."

"Neil, how about checking that wound of Jake's," John asked. "I believe I can see blood on his side."

Once assured the wounded rider was cared for, John nodded and bent over Slade to search his pockets. He unfolded a heavy piece of paper he found in the man's pocket. He struck another match to read aloud. " 'Go to the line shack nearest to Hinton. Get rid of the five men who will be there. Dispose of their bodies and their gear so they will never be found. Turn their horses loose with the herd.' " There was no signature.

He laughed. "Whoever wrote this note is going to be greatly disappointed."

Chuckling, Neil Thompson responded, "This letter sure tells us one thing, Johnny."

"What do you mean?"

"Somebody with some schooling wrote this. Willis can't write at all. I've had to write all the bills of sale for him since he started, I even have to count out the payroll for the men every month. Willis can't have written that note. In fact, I can't think of anybody in that crowd of rannys out at the Double G who could write like that, spelling the words proper and all."

"That gives us one more mystery to think about, doesn't it?" John stared at the note. "Somebody go see if you can find Slade's horse, and wait here for Bill to come back. Give him no more than an hour. If he isn't back by then come on toward Hostetter's place. If you hurry you should catch up with us."

The men wrapped Jake's wound and helped him on his horse. John carried Slade's rifle and tucked the gunfighter's pistol in one of his saddlebags. He and the three riders started toward the Hostetter Ranch. It wasn't more than an hour before the other two men joined them, each one leading a saddled horse.

It was past daybreak when John and the five riders approached the Hostetter ranch buildings. Jake was slumped over in his saddle. His wound was high up on his left side and the bullet had passed through the flesh over his ribs and out, but the wound was bleeding freely and he was weak. The group had stopped twice to re-bandage the wound, but he appeared almost ready to pass out.

Holding aloft the rifle he had taken from Slade with a white cloth tied to the end of the barrel, John muttered to himself, "I hope Alec is in the bunkhouse and that this signal he said for me to use works."

A man stepped out from the bunkhouse holding a shotgun. He had a white beard, and was stooped, but he held the shotgun steadily aimed at John's middle. "Stop where you are," he called out.

"I'm John Garrett," John said loudly. "I'm here to see Alec Gunnison. These men work for me."

The man with the shotgun studied John and the other men for a moment then answered, "I can see that you're John Garrett. Alec described you and told me to look out for you, but I wasn't expecting to see you show up with no big crowd of rannys riding with you."

"Are you telling me that Alec isn't here?" John's voice was filled with the dismay he was feeling. He dismounted to cover his confusion. "I was told he would be expecting me to join him here."

"That's exactly right, sonny. Alec's around here, but he ain't right here at the bunkhouse this very minute."

"When do you expect him back?"

"When he gets real good and ready to come back and not before, that's when I expect him."

The man lowered the shotgun but continued to scowl at John and the group of riders. He indicated the door of the bunkhouse with a nod. "Come on in, I reckon if you say so, these men are all right."

As John entered the building, he came face to face with another man holding a shotgun. "What's the matter with you men?" He placed his hands on his hips and turned to include the first man in his question.

"We've been shot at from one side and spied on from the other. We ain't been able to get a look at the bushwhacker or the spy, so we got a right to be as suspicious as we please of anybody coming around here that we don't expect," the second man answered. He appeared to be younger than the first, but he was still old. John thought both men were probably older than Alec.

"Alec will vouch for me and he knows every one of these men. He left word with Ted Bennett for me to come out here and show a white flag so you would know me." Indignation crept into John's voice. "I know he didn't expect me to show up with five other men, but these are old Double G riders, friends from six years ago when I was foreman of the ranch. They're no threat to you men or to Alec. They're only here to help.

"By the way," he continued, "you might as well know now, I gave the signal to one other man. His name is Del Ketchum. He'll be riding in here late today or tomorrow. He's working as O'Riley's deputy, but he's one of Hostetter's old riders, and he stayed around here to try to find out who back shot his boss."

The two old men rested their shotguns against the table in the center of the room. Neither man answered John or offered to introduce himself. The pair sat down at the table and picked up the cards they had evidently discarded when John and his men rode into the ranch yard. They both seemed to be determined to make a show of how unwelcome their visitors were.

Shaking his head, John took one of Jake's arms and helped support him as he crossed the room to a lower bunk. Neil Thompson helped John re-bandage Jake's wound, tightening the clean bandage over a thick pad to stop the bleeding.

"Don't be worrying about Jake, Boss. That wound's not

much more than a scratch to him." Neil turned to John. "He's tough. He'll be out of commission for a few days, but if he don't spike a fever he'll soon be up and around."

John felt relieved. He berated himself for not getting to the line shack sooner. Maybe if he had Jake wouldn't have been hurt. He looked at the other men. They were showing their weariness. He knew he had to have some sleep himself if he was going to be of any use at all.

"A couple of you men unsaddle the horses and turn them into the paddock, then get yourselves some sleep. I'll take this bunk." He tossed his hat and jacket on the bottom of the bunk next to Jake and started to climb in. "I'm sure these kind and friendly gents will warn us if we're in any danger," he added sarcastically.

The man with the white beard glared at John for a moment then turned back to his card game.

Hours later, John woke up to see the white bearded man step out of the bunkhouse door holding his shotgun against his shoulder. Jumping down from the bunk, he checked the position of his Colt and rushed to the door.

A small gray horse was just coming into view in the lane. As he reached hailing distance the man held up his rifle with a white cloth tied to the barrel. John stepped out in front of the old man and waved to Del Ketchum.

Approaching slowly, Del didn't take his eyes off of the man with the shotgun. "What's going on, John? Do you reckon you could get that guy to lower his scattergun? He's making me nervous."

John turned to the old man and said. "This man is the one I told you I was expecting. His name is Del Ketchum. He's helped me several times in the last few days, and he saved the lives of the five men who are with me, by warning me that they were going to be murdered in their sleep by Slade and his sidekick. Would you please put that shotgun away?"

The old man lowered the gun. "I don't like having seven men I don't know coming in here with only me and one other man on Alec's side. What if you fellers is lying to me?"

Just as John started to speak, he saw Alec step out of the orchard and walk up beside the bunkhouse. He waved to John and yelled to the old man holding the shotgun, "Ned Wright, will you please calm down. I know you've been spoiling for a fight, but these boys are on our side."

Alec continued walking over to grab John's hand. He grinned as he pumped it up and down and said, "I'm so glad to see you, boy. I wasn't altogether sure when I left El Paso that you would even come home. But here you are, and I noticed through the back window of the bunkhouse that you brought a small army with you."

John couldn't help but laugh. "I'm here, Alec, and I'm darn glad to finally see you. I thought sure one of these old fire-eaters would shoot somebody before the day was out."

"You're right to be wary of them, son. They're a little testy. They're good men, though. Old white beard here is Ned Wright, and the mean-looking old coot aiming the shotgun out the bunkhouse window is Jim Tilden. Ned and Jim are old friends of mine from down in Texas. I think a good part of their meanness comes from serving in the Rangers about a lifetime ago."

"It's nice to finally know their names. They never saw fit to introduce themselves to us. Let's go in the bunkhouse, Alec. I brought some of my old friends from the Double G with me. They've agreed to help us."

"I just got back from over to Blaine's place." Alec walked beside John to the bunkhouse. "He's had some more trouble. Let's go get us something to eat and I'll tell you about it."

As John and Alec stepped in the bunkhouse door, they both stopped suddenly and burst out laughing. Four men were sitting up in their bunks holding their pistols on Jim Tilden. He was still standing at the window, but he had dropped his shotgun down beside his feet.

"It's all right, boys," John said. "Put your guns away.

This gentleman is Jim Tilden, an old friend of Alec's. He wasn't really going to shoot anyone."

The four men holstered their guns. Tilden sheepishly, but carefully, picked up his shotgun and walked over to prop it against his bunk, muttering under his breath and looking at first one and then the other of the men angrily.

Alec wasted no time. He stood in the middle of the bunk-house and addressed the group. "I'm glad to see you men. It's a comfort to ride with men you know and can trust. We're going to need your guns."

He waited a moment, looking from man to man. He finally turned to John to say, "Blaine's boy got shot up bad early this morning, and right this minute there's more than twenty men hiding in that low place just south of Blaine's ranch buildings and firing at the house and bunkhouse.

"Blaine's got ten good men outside of himself, and he was smart enough to lay in a good supply of ammunition, so they can defend themselves. But with him forted up in the ranch buildings, those rannys can run off his stock. I'm afraid they might get the idea of firing the barn or even the ranch house. They don't seem to care at all that there's women in the house."

John's face turned white. *Andrea,* he thought. Fear for her made him feel sick. He knew that she would be fighting right along with her father. She could be killed at any time. "Let's go, men," he said. "Alec knows a way you can get down from the rim and work your way in behind Willis's men. Tilden and Wright can go in with you. I'm going to Blaine's house by way of the hill here.

"I need a volunteer to stay here with Jake. He can handle a gun, but he can't be expected to defend this ranch by himself if several men should decide to mount an attack." It was obvious that none of the men wanted to miss a chance to fight, so John ordered Bill Jones to stay.

He turned to Tilden and Wright. "It would be helpful if you would leave your shotguns for these two men. We've got two extra rifles if you need them."

Jim Tilden answered, "We'll leave the scatter guns,

sonny, but we don't need your rifles. We've got better guns than that little Henry you're toting."

Shaking his head at the man's prickly attitude, John left the bunkhouse. Alec and the rest of the men followed. Each man stuffed some jerky in his shirt pocket to eat as they rode, then saddled their horses and fell in behind Alec as he led off into the oak scrub at a gallop. Each man had checked his rifle. The two old rangers held Sharps 50s across the front of their saddles.

When they had ridden several miles along the edge of the hills, Alec stopped his horse, turned to face the group, and said, "Johnny, you go ahead on over to Blaine's place, I'll show these boys the way into that arroyo. We'll come out right behind those killers before they even know we're there. They won't have a chance."

John reached out to shake Alec's arm. "Be careful, old friend. I'll see you at Blaine's."

He turned to the riders. "Stick with Alec, he knows this country like the back of his hand, so he'll put you in position to stop this. I should be at the house by the time you get ready, so I can let Blaine know what's happening. I'll fire three pistol shots from the front window as the signal for you to open up on them. They'll be pinned down by a crossfire."

Nodding to the men, John turned his horse to quickly disappear into the pines. Alec and the other men spurred their horses toward the cut in the rim and the path down into the valley.

Chapter Nine

Dismounting at the edge of the pines, John opened the back door of Blaine's barn and led Prince into the dim interior. He opened the feed box and dipped some oats into a wooden bucket. Placing the horse in a stall he loosened his bridle and removed the bit so he could eat. He could go into the paddock to get water on his own, and be ready to run if John needed him.

The house seemed far away from the shelter of the barn. John decided to wait until it was full dark before he tried to make it across the backyard. He watched the gloom slowly creep down the sides of the escarpment and across the valley as he listened to the intermittent firing from the bunkhouse. The men in the slough were pretty well bunched, and making no effort to leave their place of cover. They apparently had not expected to face the kind of defense Blaine's men were putting up.

"Huh," John muttered to himself. "They're in for a nasty surprise."

Praying there was no lookout on his side of the bunkhouse, John finally bent his head and ran for the house. His boots pounded on the porch and he hit the door with his fist and yelled, "Open up, Blaine, its John Garrett."

He heard a heavy bar scrape as someone lifted it from the inside of the door. Russ Blaine opened the door and

142

grabbed John's arm, dragging him into the house. "What in blazes are you doing here!" he bellowed. "You'd be a heck of a lot more help to us out on the rim behind those buzzards than you will be trapped in here."

"Alec is leading a group of men down that gulch at the end of the pines. He should be in position to attack now. I'm going to give a signal when we're ready. How many men do you have?"

"Three were riding herd, I expect they're dead. My son was with them and he barely made it back here alive. If he hadn't gotten here to warn us we'd have been overrun before we were ready to defend ourselves. There's seven men in the bunkhouse and Julie and me in here."

"How is your son?"

"Not good." Blaine's eyes looked hopeless. "His mother's done all she can for him, and she checks on him every few minutes, but he's hurt bad. Come on out to the front of the house, Julie's alone out there."

As the two men entered the big front room, John realized that the rifle shots he heard from the kitchen were Julie Blaine's. Staying crouched down below the windows, she turned as the men approached and said, "Thank you for coming, Mr. Garrett. Alec said you would. I fear you should have stayed away."

"We have help, Mrs. Blaine. I have to signal my men." John pulled his Colt out of its holster and fired three quick shots out of the broken front window.

There was a slight pause in the shooting, then as a volley hit the front of the house; they heard firing that came from a different angle. John could hear the boom of the big Sharps rifles the two old rangers carried.

Blaine nodded grimly. "Serves the low-down snakes right."

Julie dropped her rifle and ran into the front bedroom to kneel beside her son. She had made a pallet on the floor for him to lie on to keep him safe from a stray bullet.

"I can make out the sound of men yelling, Mr. Blaine," John called from the back door. "I think we ought to go to the bunkhouse. It's closer to the slough where all the action is and we'll be stronger in a group. I don't think your wife and son will be in any danger. They'll have to get by us to reach the house."

Looking around as they headed through the kitchen, John asked, "Where is Andrea? Is she in the bunkhouse?" Sheer fright that Andrea had been hurt or killed suddenly made it hard for him to breathe.

The look on Blaine's face stopped him. "She went out this morning as usual, but she hasn't come home. I hope she heard all the shooting and just decided to stay out of the way."

"She wouldn't do that." John felt his heart sinking. "She would've come in through the pines at the back of the barn like I did."

"I'm scared to death that you're right about that, son," Blaine answered, shaking his head sorrowfully. "It seems that I may just have lost both of my children in trying to keep my ranch."

John could see that Blaine was suffering. He knew he had to finish here and go find Andrea. He and Blaine ran to the barn, then along the corral fence to the bunkhouse. Blaine started yelling as they approached. Nelson Ames opened the door and motioned them to come in. "What's happening down there? The shooting hasn't slowed down, but no firing is coming this way."

Most of the men left the windows to crowd around Blaine. Several stared at John. "Let's go down there, boys," Blaine said. "I think we can handle them now."

He turned and rushed back out the door. All of the men but John started after him with their rifles ready. John reached out and caught Blackwell's arm as he started to run past him. "Andrea may be in trouble. I'm going to ride out to the place she uses as a lookout and see if I can find her."

Blackwell looked hard at the bleak expression in the eyes of the tall man. It was plain that he was scared. "I'll go with you," he said. "It sounds as though this war is over anyway. I thought Andrea was in the house."

"Blaine said he thought she might have stayed away to keep out of the ruckus, but then he agreed with me that she would have come in the back just like I did. That girl wouldn't have hidden in the woods to keep herself safe when her family was being attacked."

Blackwell collected a horse from the corral, and while he was tying his saddle John made sure Prince had water and rearranged the bit in his mouth. Leading their horses out through the back door of the barn the two men mounted and walked the horses through the heavy brush that grew at the edge of the forest. As soon as they were far enough in the under the great pines to be out of the brush that grew along the edges where the sun could reach, they put their horses to a trot, trusting them to avoid obstacles in the gloom under the trees.

It seemed to John as though they would never get to the cabin. Their horses made little noise as they moved over the carpet of pine needles. Neither of the men tried to talk. When they finally reached the cut below the cabin, John dismounted and grabbed his rifle to lead Prince up the path toward the clearing.

After a few steps he stopped to listen, motioning to Blackwell to be still. He could hear the sound of a horse stomping its feet. Tying Prince to a nearby bush, he continued up the path toward the clearing. Blackwell was right behind him

Stopping at the edge of the open space, John whispered to Blackwell as he pointed to his left. "Work around that way and see if there's anyone in the cabin. I'm going to climb up higher. Andrea usually watches the valley from a bunch of rocks at the end of that path over there, and she may be hiding up there."

Without a word, Blackwell nodded and disappeared into the trees.

John eased around the clump of bushes near the spring and started up the escarpment. He stopped every few steps to listen. Suddenly he heard the sound of rifle fire. It seemed to be very close.

About a hundred yards above him and to the right a man cursed vilely and then yelled, "You come on down from there, Miss Blaine. This is Sheriff O'Riley talking to you. You know you've got nothing to fear from me. Your family is dead. I'll see you get to town where you'll be safe."

Cursing under his breath, John continued to creep toward the sound of the voice. As he pulled himself slowly along, he heard another, rougher voice, speaking to the sheriff in a low tone. At first he couldn't make out what was being said, then the man raised his voice a little and he could hear him clearly.

"That snip of a girl is making me mad. This is taking way too much time. I'm going to climb up there and drag her down. I seen a way I can work around behind that rock. I want her, but if I can't get her down from there soon I'll have to kill her so she can't talk."

The sheriff's voice was a pleading whine. "Rafe, you'd best know that if you harm that girl we'll both be hung. You can't be bothering women in this country. People just won't stand for it."

"I'm not worried about people. I've wanted that stuck-up little flirt since I seen her turned out in that purty white dress. I'm going to grab her. She's all that's left of the Blaines by now. I'll get that ranch legal if I marry with her. After I keep her about a week, she'll be begging me to marry her."

O'Riley and the other man continued to talk in low voices. John worked his way closer, filled with cold anger at the man's words. He heard the second man scrambling along the hillside somewhere above him. He was climbing farther up the slope, nearer the rocks where Andrea was hiding. The man must have shown himself as he moved, because another shot from Andrea's rifle pinged on a rock near his position.

John's grinned at Andrea's nerve. Suddenly, he could see the sheriff's broad back. He stood up without making a sound, and taking two quick jumps he was behind the man. Before O'Riley could turn John stuck his rifle barrel in the back of his thick neck. "Don't move, and don't make a sound, O'Riley," he whispered. "If you try to warn your friend, you're dead."

Blackwell moved up beside the two men and whispered to John, "That was well done. Do you want me to take care of the other man?"

"No. Take the sheriff on down to the cabin. He's going to live if he keeps quiet. I'll be along with his friend."

O'Riley started to speak and John pushed his rifle harder into the back of his neck. "I said for you to be quiet. Now start moving down hill."

Blackwell took over. Placing his pistol next to John's rifle barrel on the sheriff's neck he grabbed the man's arm and turned him down hill toward the cabin.

John continued climbing upward until he came to a boulder that sheltered him from the area where the other man was hiding. As soon as he was under cover he called out. "Andy, watch out to your left. One of the men is climbing up there."

Andrea didn't answer. There were no more shots. John crawled around the boulder and yelled again, "Andrea, say something so I'll know you're all right." There was still no answer. John raised up to look for the man. A bullet seemed to brush his right ear. He fell back to the ground.

Suddenly he saw Andrea pop her head and shoulders up from the group of rocks and aim her rifle toward the brush where the shot came from. She yelled at the same time she fired. "Watch yourself, John. Willis can't get up here where I am. He'd have to come out in the open and I'll kill him if he tries."

John was so relieved to hear her voice he felt weak. She sure was something. His anger at the thought of Willis daring to threaten her was growing. He wanted his hands on the man so badly, he almost felt dizzy for a moment.

"Willis," he called, striving to keep his voice steady. "It's John Garrett, why don't you come on down. Your attack on Blaine has failed. Your men are all dead or captured. You can't get away and you can't reach Andrea, so you might as well give up. We've captured Sheriff O'Riley so you're all alone."

"Forget it, Garrett," Willis growled. "Keep your distance. I'll kill you and then take the girl."

John didn't answer. He could hear the man moving. He was about fifty yards off to his right, apparently working his way back down the hill toward his own position. Keeping low, John began to advance, holding his rifle out in front of him. He was ready for Willis if he jumped him.

At the sound of rocks falling just ahead and to his left, John eased behind a boulder and tried to make himself as small a target as possible. Willis had the advantage of the high ground, but he was handicapped by having to stay down among the rocks to keep out of Andrea's sight. All was quiet.

Suddenly John caught a glimpse of the man out of the corner of his left eye. Almost at the same instant Willis landed on his back. The man lay flat on top of him. His hamlike hands went around John's neck. He heard Andrea scream, "Roll him off you, John. I can't shoot. I'm afraid I'll hit you."

John's vision was blurred. He gathered all his strength and forced his back up against Willis and jabbed him in the stomach with his elbow at the same time. Willis eased his grip on his neck just enough for John to twist away. He slammed a hard right against the side of Willis' head as he rolled out of the man's grasp.

Both men rose to their feet. Willis's face was contorted in an evil grin that said he was sure he was the stronger. He was almost the same height as John, but he was big. He probably outweighed John by forty pounds. Moving like lightning, he reached out with both hands and grabbed John's shoulders, throwing him back against the rocks. John lunged to get away and fell to the ground beside the large boulder.

Willis was beside him in an instant. For all his size the

man was amazingly fast. He swung hard with first one fist and then the other, knocking John's head from side to side. John backed him off with a quick jab to Willis's Adam's apple.

The blow to his throat must have hurt, because Willis backed up several steps, holding his throat with his right hand. John got to his feet and slammed a left into Willis's belly. As Willis fought to regain his breath John followed up with a hard kick on the side of the man's right knee.

Willis screamed and reached out to grab John's arm as he fell. He held on and slammed punches against John's side. Wrenching his arm out of Willis's grasp. John stood up and stepped away trying to get his breath. He was gasping with pain in his ribs. He shook his head to try to clear it.

Willis got to his feet and rushed at him. He grabbed for John's throat with one hand. Ducking away, John felt himself falling backward. He rolled as he landed, and Willis' boot missed his head inches. John lunged upright as another vicious kick glanced off the side of his head. Dizzy with pain, he grabbed Willis's arms and hung on desperately, trying to clear his head. Willis pushed John away so hard he almost fell. He followed up with a vicious swing that missed then he landed a left jab that cut John's cheek to the bone.

John slammed a right to Willis's mouth and followed it with a left to his ribs. Blood was dripping from Willis's chin, but he shook his head and kept swinging. John ducked a nasty swipe with Willis's right and slammed another solid blow to the man's stomach. Willis bent over with pain, and John followed up with a hard right aimed at the cut on Willis's mouth.

John ducked Willis's next blow, but a powerful right connected alongside his head and he went back on his heels. Willis tried closing in, but John struck him hard with his right. He heard bone crunch in Willis's nose.

The big man staggered back and almost fell. Coming back at John again, he began to just throw punches without any direction. John struck hard with both fists, connecting with Willis's face and then hammering his midsection. Willis's knees buckled, and then he fell to the ground. John stepped back.

At that moment Blackwell stepped up behind Willis and stuck his pistol against the back of his neck. "I enjoyed the fight, but I think you've both had enough fun for today."

"I thought you were going to stand back there and let that big lummox kill me," John said, rubbing the side of his face. His right eye was almost shut. Blood was running down his neck from the cut on his cheek. His head was buzzing from the force of the blows he had taken.

Blackwell prodded Willis with the gun. "Keep still, you yellow polecat. Get me that rope yonder on that rock, John. I want this piece of dirt tied up so tight he can't even think of escaping."

Pulling himself together John climbed up toward the rock where Andrea was sheltered. "It's me, Andrea," he called.

The girl jumped from the rock almost in his arms. He grabbed her and held her tight against his chest. "Lord, girl," he whispered. "I was scared to death."

After a moment she pulled back from his embrace. Smiling up into his eyes she said, "I'm kind of glad to see you. Even if you are all bloody. I only had three bullets left. I was figuring on trying to run when I saw you creeping up from the spring. I thought at first that you were with those rats."

"Oh, John." She stopped talking for a moment and looked horrified. She reached up and touched John's right cheek. "Oh, your poor face."

"I'll heal. I've been hit before."

"Please tell me about my family. Are they all right?"

"Your father and mother are safe. Alec and I brought in some riders and broke up the fight. Did you know your brother was wounded?"

"Oh no. Is he hurt bad?" John's expression alerted her that the wound was serious. "John, tell me. Is he alive?"

"He was when I left, but your father and mother didn't seem to think he would make it."

"If he dies it will kill Mama."

"Let's go. We can't find out how Billy is until we get back to the ranch. Blackwell is down at the clearing with Willis and the sheriff. I guess we have to figure out what to do with them. I know we'll have to protect them from your father after we tell him what happened to you up here."

"You may have to protect them both from me." Andrea shuddered as she spoke. "I knew I didn't like O'Riley, but I could hardly believe it when I realized he was helping that brute Rafe Willis."

"Where's your pony?"

"Down on the flat below the cabin. Willis killed him. That's how they trapped me up here. They were waiting for me in that little patch of cottonwoods where you cross the creek. My pony warned me they were there, so I got past them. They chased me. I was going to lose them in the pines, but they shot my horse. The only thing I could do then was run up here into the rocks where I could defend myself."

"Prince will carry double," John said, placing his hands around his mouth he called, "Hey Blackwell. I'll take care of Willis, you get the sheriff and let's go."

Blackwell popped into view from the direction of the cabin. He had obviously been lurking in the edge of the woods listening to their conversation. "He's right here beside Willis. They began to howl so much when I tied their hands properly that I had to gag the snakes to shut them up."

Leading the sheriff and Willis by a rope around each man's neck, Blackwell entered the clearing. In addition to tying their hands behind them, he had stuffed a rag in each man's mouth and wrapped a handkerchief around their faces to hold them in place. The sheriff looked at Blackwell as though he could kill.

Blackwell ignored the man's looks and simply yanked

on the rope to keep the men moving along. "I've asked this big ox where his horse is several times, but he just stares at me," Blackwell said. "I even gave him permission to nod his head in the right direction, but he's just an uncooperative person. I reckon he'll just have to walk behind my horse all the way back to Hinton."

The sheriff moaned through the gag. Chuckling, John walked over and untying the handkerchief from around O'Riley's face he pulled the rag out of his mouth.

"You son-of-a—"

Placing a hand over the sheriff's mouth, John snarled. "Don't say a thing but where your horses are O'Riley, or I'll tie this gag back on your sorry face and let this man do anything he likes to you."

It seemed that O'Riley's face grew even redder, and if possible, his eyes got meaner, but he answered through set teeth, "He's tied about two hundred yards below that cabin in the edge of the trees."

Blackwell waited where he was for John to bring both their horses. Mounting, he walked his horse back into the trees toward the cabin. He was still leading the sheriff by the rope around his neck.

John lifted Andrea onto Princes saddle and mounted behind her. He followed Blackwell down the path, holding the rope tied around Willis's neck in his left hand.

When they reached Willis and O'Riley's horses, John dismounted and helped Blackwell tie the sheriff's feet together under his horse's belly and his hands to the saddle horn. Blackwell took the reins to lead the horse. He kept the rope tied around the man's neck. They repeated the process with Willis.

As they prepared to leave Blackwell called to John, "Do you think there's a tree close to the ranch where we can hang these two?"

"Take it easy now, Blackwell. We're going to take these men in to Hinton and lock them up in the sheriff's own jail. Then we're going to wire a United States Marshall to decide what to do with them."

"That doesn't seem enough for what they tried to do," Ames said. He yanked viciously on the rope around O'Riley's neck and started his horse straight across the open range toward the ranch buildings.

Andrea was silent. She rode with her head down, her hands wrapped around the saddle horn. John knew she was afraid of what she would find when they reached the ranch. He held her close to his chest.

Men seemed to be everywhere in the yard between the Blaine ranch buildings and the house. Dead and injured men had been loaded in two wagons, ready for the trip to Hinton. A group of men sat their saddles with their hands and feet securely tied. They hung their heads dolefully.

Blaine whooped when he saw Andrea and ran to her side. She fell off the horse into his arms. As Blaine took her into house, John and Ames added O'Riley and Willis to the group of mounted prisoners.

Blackwell removed the ropes from O'Riley's and Willis's necks, and secured their horses to those of the other prisoners. Sandy Miller shook hands with John and Blackwell and asked, his voice trembling with anger, "Is Miss Andy all right? Did those low-down buzzards harm her?"

"They never touched her, Sandy," John assured him. "She hid in the rocks and held them off with her rifle until we got there."

"Those lowdown, sorry—. They're dead men. Don't they know that every decent man in the territory will be out to kill them?"

"They thought you and Blaine and the whole outfit would be killed in the raid on the ranch. If you had been there wouldn't have been anyone left to go after them. Blackwell and I heard O'Riley trying to lure Andrea down by telling her that her family was killed and she was all alone. He was telling her he would protect her and all the time he was just that beast Willis's shill. He thought they were safe."

"Well, he thought wrong. We were almost ready to head

to town with this load of trash. I know Nelson Ames wants to go, but I don't expect Blackwell will. Are you able to ride with us, John?" Sandy was staring at the bruises on John's face.

"I feel a lot better than I look. Tell me what happened in the shooting fight. Did we lose any men?"

"None. Only person who caught a bullet is Alec, but he's all right."

"Where is he? How was he hurt?" John asked anxiously.

"He's in the bunkhouse, he only got a little nick on his arm. That white-bearded friend of his insisted he had to bind it up."

"I'll see what Alec thinks we should do about the Double G now that we have most of its crew shot up or tied on a horse. I have to find out what's happened over there with my father."

"There's a wounded guy over there in the wagon by the name of Will Simmons. He's been talking some. He claims he didn't sign on for some of the things that have been going on around here. He would like us to believe that he was only with the crew that attacked the ranch because he was afraid if he tried to leave Willis or one of the others would shoot him."

"Knowing what I do about Rafe Willis, that actually sounds reasonable to me. I'll ride with you men into Hinton, and maybe I can get to talk with Simmons away from the others." John replied.

John went over to Blackwell and offered his hand in thanks for his part in rescuing Andrea.

"Tell me about Blaine's son," John asked Sandy Miller as they prepared to leave. "Is he still alive?"

"Blaine just told us a few minutes ago that the boy seems to be stronger, and so far he has no fever. He gave us orders to bring the Doc back to the ranch with us. It won't take him but a few minutes to finish patching up these wounded men. Then he'll be able to leave to come out here. Miz Blaine has already bandaged their hurts, and she's a better doctor than most."

John was glad to see Alec and the two rangers come out of the bunkhouse. "Go on to Hinton with Miller, John," he said, "and make sure somebody in town takes charge of this bunch of murdering varmints."

"I'll take your Double G riders back to Hostetter's place with us so we can all rest up a little. You come get us when you're ready to go to the ranch. According to what that Simmons fella there says a few of Willis's trash is still hanging around over there. We need to clear them out before this mess will be completely over." Without stopping, Alec waved good-bye and entered the barn to get his horse.

The trip to Hinton took hours. John was so tired he dozed in the saddle three or four different times. He noticed that several of the men around him were doing the same thing. Idly, he counted eleven mounted prisoners, and only four in the wagon carrying the wounded. There was a canvas covering the wagon that carried the dead men. He couldn't count them, but the wagon appeared to be full. Alec, the two old rangers, and the other men had counted a terrible toll on Willis's gunslingers.

The Blaine cowboys had tied the mounted prisoners horses together to make it more difficult for any of them to get away. Two of the riders had followed Blackwell's idea and led the group with ropes tied around a man's neck. One of those men was Rafe Willis, and the other was Sheriff O'Riley.

Men and women ran out of stores and houses to watch as the strange cavalcade rolled into Hinton. John and Sandy Miller had moved forward to ride at the front of the group. Several people recognized John and yelled hello to him. Right behind John and Sandy's horses were the wagons. The first one carried the bodies of the men who were killed in the fight. They were covered, but it wasn't hard to see that the canvas covered several bodies.

Next in line was the wagon that held the wounded men. Two men sat at the front leaning against back of the seat. Two others were lying in the wagon bed. They had been roughly bandaged, but their clothes were bloody, attesting to the seriousness of their wounds. Behind the wagons were the mounted prisoners. Del Ketchum and Nelson Ames led them. Ames periodically gave the rope tied around Sheriff's O'Riley's neck a vicious yank. Another Blaine cowboy held the rope that was tied around Willis' neck. By the time they reached the front of the sheriff's office and jail, the sidewalks were lined with amazed townspeople.

Just as they reached the front of the jail Ted Bennett stepped around the building and out onto board sidewalk. He stood with his hands on his hips and a big grin on his face as he watched John and Sandy Miller dismount.

"Has there been a war?" he asked.

"That's the only thing you could call it," John answered. "These rannys attacked the Blaine ranch, shot up some of their riders, and severely wounded Bill Blaine. Russ Blaine and his men held them off until Alex Gunnison and some of local men sneaked up behind them and turned the tables."

"Was the sheriff with them?"

"Our sheriff is a special case. He was sort of with them at first, but he left to take care of a private job. When we caught him he was halfway up the north rim above Silver Creek trying to help Willis capture Blaine's girl, Andrea. We heard him telling the girl that all of her family was dead, so he knew exactly what was happening down at the ranch. We also heard him tell her that he would protect her, but he was just acting as a decoy to help Willis get his dirty hands on the girl."

The bystanders who could hear what John was saying began to talk among themselves in angry voices. They were obviously less than pleased to think that their sheriff would try to help Willis capture a young girl. A man in front of the saloon yelled, "Let's hang the low-down buzzards."

Ted Bennett and the two old rangers stepped forward. Bennett reached for the rope tied around the sheriff's neck and said, "Let's get this scum into the jail, fellas. We don't need any problems here."

Del Ketchum used his key to open the door to the

sheriff's office and the jail. There were no prisoners in the two cells, but the eleven uninjured men quickly filled them. As soon as the cell doors were locked, Ketchum and Bennett came back out to the sheriff's office and locked the heavy door leading to the cellblock.

"Will you wire the United States marshall to come handle this mess, Ted?" Del Ketchum asked.

"You're the sheriff now, Del, it's your place to do that," Bennett answered.

"I don't know if people will accept me taking O'Riley's place. I've gone along with what-all he's done for over a year. Some of them folks are giving me real hard looks. I can't say I blame them much for thinking bad of me. They've got no way of knowing that I've not hurt anybody. I've even been able to prevent a few bad things from happening, but I can't expect them to believe that on my say so."

"Just take the job, Del. There's not a soul who will question you if Johnny and Alec and I support you. The town has to have someone in charge here. I'll go see if Johnny and Sandy Miller found the doctor."

A huge crowd had gathered in the street when Bennett came out of the sheriff's office. He stopped to watch as the undertaker pushed his way through the crowd and lifted the canvas on the wagon to count seven dead men. Shaking his head, the man didn't speak but walked around the wagon and climbed on the high seat. Turning the horses, he guided them through the mass of people.

As Bennett stepped out onto the sidewalk Asa Hamilton ran across the street from the bank and called to him frantically. "What's going on here, Bennett? Why are all these people crowding around here? Who were all those wounded men in the other wagon?"

"Hey. Slow down Asa. I can't answer but one question at a time. What's going on is a bunch of those gunmen of Willis's tried to take over the Blaine ranch and got shot up for their trouble."

"Oh no," Hamilton said, looking sick. "I thought I saw

Sheriff O'Riley tied on his horse. I can't believe that crowd of men had the nerve to tie up a sheriff. How did that come about?"

"O'Riley helped Willis try to kidnap Blaine's girl and got caught at it. He's lucky he didn't get a rope before they made it to town."

"That can't be right. There has to be some mistake. I can't believe he would be fool enough to do that."

"There's no mistake, Hamilton. Johnny Garrett and another man caught them in the act. They slipped up behind the sheriff and heard him talking to Willis. Willis was raving about what all he was going to do to the girl when he caught her. O'Riley was with the men who raided Blaine's ranch too, because the same men heard him tell the Blaine girl that her folks were all dead and he would protect her. All the time he was hiding behind a rock with Willis."

"What are we going to do for a sheriff?"

"That's all taken care of. Del Ketchum has been deputy sheriff for a good year now. He's taking over."

"Ted, you know you can't let that happen. Why, Del Ketchum knows too much, and Willis told me not to trust him. You have to get rid of him. He'll ruin everything. This is ridiculous." Hamilton's face was red and he was beginning to sound almost hysterical.

"I'm the mayor, Asa," Bennett said quietly. "I have the authority and I know what I'm doing. I say Del serves as sheriff until we can have an election. He's on his way to wire the U.S. Marshall's office now. I think maybe I'll go tell him he should wire the circuit judge while he's at it."

Bennett leaned nearer to the banker and spoke softly so no one but the banker could hear him. "You know, Asa, you and Willis are the only ones who have broken any laws so far." Not waiting for Hamilton to say anything more he turned away and proceeded down the street to the Western Union office.

Hamilton stood as if frozen in place and stared after Bennett as he walked away from him along the boardwalk. He thought about what could happen to him if there were a

United States Marshall in town, nosing into things. Especially since Bennett was acting so strangely. Suddenly starting as if he had been struck, Hamilton turned and almost ran back across the street and into the front door of the bank.

John stepped out of the doctor's office just as Bennett was passing. "Hey, Ted. This is really something, isn't it?"

"That's a fact. Let's have a drink. You can tell me all about it."

The two men made their way through the thinning crowd to the saloon. Several men John had known most of his life came over to the bar and shook his hand. He greeted them cordially, but refused to be drawn into a discussion of the fight at Blaine's ranch, or the capture of the sheriff.

"I told Del to go ahead and act as sheriff," Bennett said as they took their drinks to a table. "He'll probably have to prove himself to some of the people in town, after serving as O'Riley's deputy for almost a year, but I'll vouch for him, and I'm sure you will as well."

"He's proven himself to me," John said. "He saved the lives of several of my men by warning me when the sheriff and Willis were planning to have them murdered in cold blood. He also found out that the banker, Asa Hamilton, is mixed up in this mess some way or another."

"What in the world did he find out about Hamilton?" Bennett asked in a surprised voice. He dropped his eyes as he waited for John to answer.

"He saw Willis sneak in the door of Hamilton's office in the back of the bank several nights. It was after dark each time. He appeared to be extremely careful not to let anyone see him. Ketchum said he saw him go in there five or six different nights and stay for a couple of hours. Three or four of those times, the sheriff joined them. He thought there was another man there as well on a least two nights, but he never could find out who that fella was."

"That does look strange doesn't it. It pretty well tells us that Ketchum is clean too, don't you think?" Bennett asked.

"You know that Del stayed here in Hinton to try to find

out who killed Hostetter. All you have to do is let the town council and a few other men know that, and he won't have any trouble being accepted as sheriff."

"I'll make sure to do that at the very next town council meeting." Bennett finished his beer and motioned for the bartender to refill his glass. "By the way, Elaine Hostetter telegraphed me that she will be back here sometime this week. I wired her that you were back in town and explained how things were shaping up. I thought she should know. I think we're going to find out who killed her husband."

"You sounded mighty pleased when you said she was coming back, am I missing something?" John smiled at the tone of Bennett's voice.

"I sound pleased? Yeah, I guess I am pleased. I've always had a soft spot for Elaine. She's quite a lady. I would have let her know how I felt before she left, but I just couldn't say anything to her when she had just buried her husband."

"Why, I'm surprised, Ted." John smiled. "You sound serious. I've always pictured you as a crusty old bachelor lawyer, maybe even a circuit judge, traveling around the territory, with no time for a wife."

"Well, you pictured wrong." Bennett chuckled. "I'll let Elaine know how I feel as soon as she gets here and then leave it up to her. I enjoy my comforts, that's a fact, but I'll marry her if she'll have me."

"I have to go." John stood up. "If I don't eat and get some sleep, I'll fall over. Alec and I are going out to the Double G tomorrow. I have to find out what's happened to my father."

"Since Del will have to stay here to take care of the prisoners, I'll go out there with you if it's all right with you. There are several of your father's old friends here in town that will want to ride with you as well. They've heard the talk that he might be dead or disabled in some way."

"Ketchum says he saw my father through the window of the ranch house," John replied. "He caught a glimpse of him lying back in that Morris chair of his. That seems to say to me that he's sick or hurt. As I told you the other day, that's the only explanation I can accept. Pa and I have had our differences, but he wouldn't be any part of back-shooting Hostetter or shooting Blaine's men down from ambush. He wouldn't have ordered that raid on Blaine's ranch either."

Bennett went with John as he left the saloon and walked beside him along the boardwalk toward the hotel. Just as they started to enter the hotel, two men ran out of the bank. One was yelling, "Help, help, somebody, the bank's been robbed!"

"Go see what's up John, I'll go get Del." Bennett ran back down the boardwalk to the front of the sheriff's office calling Del Ketchum's name.

"What do you want?" Ketchum asked as he cracked open the door with his gun in his hand.

"The bank's been robbed."

"Stay here and watch the prisoners, Bennett," Del ordered as he holstered his gun and ran across the street to enter the bank right behind John Garrett and the two men who had given the alarm. He shut the front door of the bank behind him and locked it.

"What happened here?" he demanded, turning to the two men who were pacing up and down behind the teller's cages and wringing their hands.

"Hamilton cleaned out the safe and left. We didn't notice it for a while, but later we needed some extra cash and when we opened the safe it was empty."

"How do you know Hamilton left?" Ketchum asked.

One of the men stepped forward. "I looked out the back window and saw him leave. He and his wife were riding in that big buckboard of his. They had two big trunks tied on the back. They went through the gate at the back of his house and turned toward Smithville. He was using a whip to push his horses. I didn't think anything of it at the time. Hamilton always was impatient and in a hurry."

"Mitchell, you're the head teller, you take charge here," Ketchum ordered. "I guess the first thing for you to do is figure out how much money is missing. I'll go after Hamilton. John, you help Bennett keep the folks in town calm, I'll be back."

"You can't do this alone, Del," John argued.

"The devil I can't. I won't even kill the son-of-a-gun. I'd rather bring him back and give him to the people he stole from. He's got a lot of explaining to do, and it won't be just about robbing the bank either."

After almost an hour of assuring panicked townspeople that Del Ketchum would catch up with Hamilton and retrieve their money, John finally made it to his hotel room. He propped a chair under the door handle and fell on the bed with his clothes on. He was asleep as soon as his head hit the pillow.

Chapter Ten

Shouts and screams were coming from the street. John felt disoriented and confused. He sat up on the edge of the bed. He hadn't been dreaming, he could still hear the bedlam going on outside his window. He pulled the curtain aside and looked out. Del Ketchum was coming down the street walking and leading his horse. Asa Hamilton was tied in the saddle. Hamilton had a white bandage around his head and one arm in a sling. The handles of a satchel were hooked over the saddle horn.

Pulling on his boots as fast as he could and grabbing his hat, John removed the chair from his door and ran out into the hallway. In the few minutes it took him to get downstairs and out in front of the hotel, Del had made it to the sheriff's office and was dragging Hamilton down off his horse.

Bennett ran out of the office with a scattergun and grabbed Hamilton's good arm, to drag him inside. "You people stay back!" he yelled, waving the muzzle of the shotgun at the growing crowd of angry townspeople that kept pushing forward, trying to get their hands on the banker.

"Take it easy, folks," Del said as he moved to stand in front of the closed office door. "I got your money back, every last cent of it. If you will just calm down, I'll take it over to Sam Mitchell at the bank and he'll make sure everything is there. Go on about your business."

A voice from the crowd jeered, "Why in blazes should we do what you say, Ketchum?"

Dell turned toward the voice and said loudly, "Because the mayor made me acting sheriff, and if any one of you harm a prisoner of mine you'll join him in jail to wait for the circuit judge. Is that plain enough for you?"

Some of the men grumbled to each other, but no one seemed to want to challenge him. Del watched the crowd for a few minutes, then stepped into the office, closed the door behind him and locked it. He went over to the opening in the inside door and looked in. Bennett had locked Hamilton in one of the cells that were already crowded with prisoners. The banker sat on the floor with his head in his hands.

"Tell me what happened, Del," Bennett asked as he hung the key ring beside the office door.

"There's little enough to tell. I caught up with Hamilton quicker than I expected. He had taken the old road, thinking to escape that way, but that little creek near Nolan's place had washed the road out and he couldn't get the buckboard through. He had to go back to the cut-off and take the main road. When I caught up with him the fool pulled a pistol and shot at me. I shot back. That little scrape on his shoulder knocked him off the buckboard. That's how he got that bump on his head. When he hit the ground he started screaming and gave up.

"His poor wife was hysterical by the time I got to the buckboard. When she had calmed down some she wrapped up Hamilton's wounds and showed me where the bank money was hidden. Hamilton had put it in this valise and stuck it in one of the trunks tied to the back of the buckboard.

"I asked her if she wanted to come back to town or go on to Smithville where she could catch a stage out of the territory. She sort of collapsed down in the dirt and sat there and cried for a few minutes, then she looked up at me and said she would have to come back to town, because she didn't have any money.

"After I thought about that for a few minutes, I opened up one of the bank bags and took two thousand dollars of that money out and gave it to her. She gave me a wild look, but she didn't say thank you or good-bye or nothing. She just grabbed that money, climbed up on the seat of that buckboard, and whipped up the horses. I reckon she's reached Smithville and is safely on a stage by now."

Bennett chuckled. "You don't have to say anything about Mrs. Hamilton to anybody else, Del. Just tell any body that asks that she had nothing to do with Hamilton's business and has left the country. That's surely the truth as far as it goes. I'll tell the men at the bank what happened to the two thousand dollars. Part of that money probably really did belong to Hamilton."

"Thanks, Mr. Bennett," Del replied with a grin. "I appreciate that."

Bennett answered a knock at the door. John Garrett entered and said, "Good work Del, you'll be the town's hero now. You'll never have any trouble getting anyone in this town to support you for sheriff after this."

John turned to Bennett. "Come have something to eat with me, Ted. I've got to leave town in about half an hour. Nelson Ames has gone on out to Hostetter's and I'm going to meet the men at the ranch turnoff."

"I'm going with you, John. You go ahead and get you some food and I'll meet you at the livery."

Bennett and six other men were sitting their horses in front of the livery stable when John walked around the corner. John looked at the lined faces of his father's old friends. The owner of the hotel nodded a greeting but did not speak. James Otis, the editor of the newspaper, had the butt end of a Sharps fifty-caliber rifle resting on his right knee. The other men were also heavily armed.

John was astounded. He stopped and nodded to the men. When he finally found his voice, he said, "Thank you for coming, men. I know my father will be honored by your loyalty."

The six men were gray haired, but they were western men, toughened by building a life in a place where every one had experienced using a gun to defend him self and the people he loved. Otis was the oldest, he had lost an arm at Chancellorsville serving with the Confederate forces when he was less than twenty years old. Tim Walker, the owner of the hotel had fought with Grant in Tennessee. The rest of the men were also from the elder Garrett's generation, but they were good fighting men who would be valuable if the rest of Willis's riders attempted to keep them off the double G.

Bennett had Prince saddled and ready. John stopped beside the horse long enough to add several boxes of ammunition to his saddlebag and then mounted to lead the group out of town.

Nelson Ames, Alec and twelve other men were waiting where the lane that led to Hostetter's ranch turned off the main road. They were all armed with rifles and handguns. The two ex-rangers carried their shotguns across their laps and had their Sharps in their saddle boots. Without stopping to talk, John waved for them to join the men riding with him and headed on toward the Double G.

As soon as they were within rifle range of the bunkhouse, John had the men dismount and leave their horses. "Keep your heads down," he warned. He expected to meet gunfire when they approached the buildings, but all was silent. The ranch appeared to be deserted.

When the men reached the fence alongside the main corral John motioned for them to hold back. "Tell the men to stay here where you can get to some cover if someone starts shooting," he whispered to Ames. Without waiting for a reply he walked on toward the bunkhouse, his rifle ready.

John stopped about a hundred yards from the bunkhouse. The door was standing open. Something about it gave him an eerie feeling. Holding his Henry ready, he approached the open door. Suddenly, he heard the zing and thump of a bullet hitting the dirt near his feet. The shot had come from the ranch house. John lowered the rifle and ran the rest of the way to the bunkhouse. He fell into the open door.

He heard several answering shots from his men, then everything went quiet again. Still sitting on the floor, John looked around the large room. At first he thought the building was empty, but he could hear a noise coming from the direction of the foreman's quarters. Keeping below the windows so the rifleman in the house couldn't see him, he approached the room cautiously. Someone was moaning. He stepped through the door and into the room holding his rifle ready.

Two men were lying on the floor in the far corner of the room. They were tied hand and foot. Both men had a gag in his mouth. John recognized one of the men as a former rider of Hostetter's. He assumed from the apron he wore that the second man was the cook. He lowered his rifle and used his knife to cut the ropes from around each man's feet, then quickly freed their hands and arms. The men lost no time pulling the gags from their faces.

"I'm John Garrett, Mason Garrett's son. Can you tell me what's happening here?" He asked as he helped the men to their feet.

Both of the men looked relieved. The man in the apron answered. "All of Willis's gun slicks took off night before last. When things got hot in the raid over to Silver Creek Ranch, Andy Bell run out on the rest of them. He come busting in here in a wild panic. When he told the men that were in the bunkhouse what was happening over to Blaine's place, those rannys were ready to ride. When they left here they were planning to head on out to the western range and pick up most of Garrett's market herd on their way to the badlands. Andy Bell sort of took charge and said everybody should pack up as fast as they could."

"Jilly and I didn't want any parts of that bunch. Bell could see that me and Jilly here won't packing up to go nowhere, so he just give us a hard look and went outside.

In a few minutes Poag Schmidt come in here and whispered to us that Bell had sent him to kill us, but he was going to tie us up so we couldn't make no trouble until they was out of the country."

The second man spoke then. "Poag owed me. I had pulled him from under a downed horse some years back, and he knew me and Jack here were good friends. Even killers pays their debts sometimes, I reckon.

"He kind of lagged behind the other fellas and tied us up so's we couldn't move, then he threw a couple of shots out the window and left. I guess he told them he killed us, because nobody come back in the bunkhouse to check up on us. We heard the whole bunch ride away."

"Is Del Ketchum with you?" the man called Jack asked.

"No, he had to stay in Hinton. He's acting sheriff. The men who raided Russ Blaine's ranch kind of got the wrong end of the stick. Rafe Willis and Sheriff O'Riley tried to capture Blaine's girl while the fight at Silver Creek was going on. They got caught and now and they're sitting in the Hinton jail hoping the United States Marshall and the Circuit Judge will get there before some of the townspeople take them out and lynch them."

John looked up to see Ames, Alec, and several other men climbing in the back windows of the bunkhouse holding their rifles ready to shoot. They stopped and stared at the two strange men. "I can vouch for these men," John said, placing a hand on the shoulder of the man called Jilly. "I remember when Jack here rode for Hostetter and he spoke up for this man. One of Willis's men tied and gagged them both before they rode out of here."

Turning to Ames and Alec, John continued. "I still don't know who it could be that fired that shot from up at the house."

"How do you suggest we get in the house?" Ames asked.

"That won't be any problem," John replied. "We can leave most of the men here in the bunkhouse and work our way around those bushes right close to the back of the house until we get to the cellar door. It's easy to get inside from there."

Crouching low and hoping he wouldn't be seen by the rifleman in the house, John ran the few feet over to the bushes that ran along the side and rear of the house then proceeded toward the cellar door. He could hear Ames and two other men close behind him. The double doors that covered the entrance to the cellar were held fast by a heavy oak board that had been slipped down between two stout brackets. He pulled the board up out of the brackets and dropped it on the ground. Opening one of the double doors, he stepped down into the darkness.

John counted the ten steps to the dirt floor. He struck a match, looking for the lantern that should have been hanging near the foot of the steps. It took the third match to find it, hanging on a nail up near the top of the stairs where a door opened into the kitchen. When the match went out he climbed the stairs on his hands and knees and groped along the wall until he found the lantern. Once he got the lantern burning he motioned for the men waiting at the bottom of the stairs to follow as he got ready to open the door to the kitchen.

The door to the kitchen resisted his first push, but he knew it was only held shut by a wooden block. He backed down one step and hit the door with his shoulder. The door flew open and he stumbled into the kitchen. Righting himself, he held his rifle ready as he looked around the big room.

Close behind him Ames whispered, "This place looks deserted, Johnny. The stove's cold, and there ain't no water in the bucket."

"Take it easy. Somebody shot at me from this house. They didn't have to be in the kitchen. In fact, I'm pretty sure the shot came from upstairs.

"You men stay close," John whispered as he started down the hall. "If we split up to search we might accidentally shoot each other."

The men moved from room to room as a group. The

house was an unbelievable mess. It looked as though some-one had searched each room while trying to leave as much chaos as possible. Pieces of furniture were turned over in the middle of the floor, some were smashed, their legs bro-ken off and thrown across the room. Books were pulled out of their shelves and thrown around, many had pages torn out. Rugs were rolled up. Curtains had been yanked down from windows.

"I wonder what the blasted varmint was looking for?" asked Ames, shaking his head at the destruction.

"It almost looks like they were just tearing up the house," John said. "Let's look in the office. If the old man had anything valuable in the house he would have kept it hid-den in there somewhere."

The office was more of a mess than the other rooms if that was possible. Papers were all over the floor. The big Morris chair that Mason Garrett loved to sit in was pushed against a wall in the corner. Suddenly, John knew what Del Ketchum had seen that he thought was the old man, and his heart sank. A plaid shirt his father often wore was draped over the back of the chair. It was topped by a small piece of snow-white cloth. From this viewpoint it was ob-vious that no one was in the chair, but Del had gotten only a glimpse and that was from a distance. Someone had de-liberately made it look as though his father was in the house. That he was still alive.

"I'll look in here later, fellas." John strained to keep his voice steady. "It may be that some of these papers thrown around the floor will be a help in understanding what's been happening around here."

Ames took the lead as the group of men went upstairs, taking the steps as quietly as possible. When they reached the upper landing John immediately noticed the narrow door to the attic. "Check the bedrooms carefully, you men," he whispered as he eased the door open. "I'll go look up here."

As he started to climb up the narrow staircase, a head appeared at the top. It was their Mexican housekeeper. "Señor Johnny, is that really you?" She almost sobbed the words.

"Come on down, Elena. It's really me. You're perfectly safe. Willis and all of his men are gone." John grinned up at the woman who had been like a mother to him most of his life. He reached up to hug her, then taking her arm he helped her down the attic stairs.

"Stop crying and talk to me, Elena. Was it you who fired the rifle at me?"

"*Sí, mi hijo,* I fired the rifle. I did not know it was you. I only had one bullet. The rifle was your old one. It was in the trunk in the attic. I found one shell in the bottom of the trunk. I was afraid you were those men coming back."

"Tell me where my father is, Elena." John kept his arm around the small woman as he led her out into the upper hall. Ames and the three men following him stood back and grinned at each other as they remembered the care they had taken approaching a house defended by this less than formidable adversary.

Elena dropped her head into her hands and began to sob again.

"Stop crying, Elena," John said sternly. "I must know."

"*El patron . . . su padre, es muerto.*"

"Talk English, Elena," John admonished the woman sternly, "and tell us what happened."

"Your father left the house with Willis. They went to the salt lick near the old Spanish mine. My Esteban rode with them. He was on the other side of the lick where no one could see him. He heard your father and Willis yelling at each other, but he could not understand their words. Their voices were so angry that Esteban grew frightened. He hid himself in the rocks and watched.

"Willis knocked the *patron* from his horse. He hit his head when he fell. Esteban did not know if he was dead then, but he lay still as if he were dead. Two of your old riders, the two Simpson brothers, saw your father fall. They rushed up to face Willis. He did not speak. He just shot them.

"Willis called to several of his new riders. When they came out where Esteban could see their faces. That banker Hamilton and another town man was with them. Hamilton put his hand on the Patron's neck and shook his head. Two of the men lifted your father and carried him to the opening of the old mine. They pulled away two of the boards that were over the opening and pushed your father inside. They went back and got the bodies of the Simpsons and pushed them inside as well.

"Esteban was afraid. He hid in the rocks until the men left. They knew he had ridden out from the ranch with them, and he was sure they would know that he had seen what they did, so he stayed in the hills. He finally sneaked into town and sent the *vieja* who lives in the shack behind the cantina and sells simples out here to tell me. She pretended to be selling me a cure for . . . for . . . *una problema . . . yo no se.* She whispered to me what Esteban saw at the mine."

John patted Elena's hand. "Go rest, Elena. I'll go to the mine. Lock the doors to the house and go and sleep. We'll be back."

John sent all of the men except Ted Bennett and the other men from town westward toward the back ranges of the Double G. "The herd would have been down in that bowl near Black creek, I expect," he said. "They couldn't make much time pushing nearly a thousand cows. Just stay behind them. Stay back far enough so they won't know you're following. They'll take the herd to the nearest place they can sell it for cash and pretend they're driving for my father. That will likely be Smithville. The only other possibility is the Army post. You'll soon know which way they are headed.

"We'll catch up with you in a few hours. We'll decide when we get there when to take the herd away from them."

John stood still and watched the men mount up and ride away, then he mounted Prince and led Bennett and the other men toward the old Spanish mine and his father's body. His mind felt paralyzed. Thinking seemed impossible. He had convinced himself that his father was surely dead, that he had to be dead for things to be happening the way they were, but he suddenly found that thinking his father was dead and knowing it for sure were vastly different things.

He and the old man had fought, mostly with words ever since he was a smart-aleck kid who thought he knew everything. They had even come to blows the last time his father had tried to whip him, but to know he was dead. That felt unreal. It didn't seem possible.

Pictures suddenly formed in John's mind of his father's body rolling down the slope of the mine entrance. Swelling in the heat. Then he imagined his arms and legs torn by animals. He shook his head to clear it. He knew there would be mostly bones left when they found the body. He only hoped there would be enough left of the men's clothes to absolutely identify them.

As they rode, John resolved that he and his party would confirm that the bodies were in the mineshaft, then they would go on to catch up with the men chasing the cattle. After they returned to the ranch with the herd he would have some men take a wagon and three coffins to gather up what was left of the men and bring them back to the ranch to bury.

It took more than an hour to reach the hills and the salt lick. Skirting the pits and pools of brackish water and the slick areas where animals had come to lick the salty clay around them, the group of men approached the rocky area near the hidden entrance to the mine.

One of the heavy timbers that had closed the adit was lying on the ground. Forcing himself not to think about his father, John reached in his saddlebag for a pair of leather gloves to protect his hands.

"Wait until I clear the opening to the mine, Ted. We have to be careful. I remember that the floor slopes away sharply for about ten yards before it levels out. I expect the bodies rolled down to the level area."

After removing the last two timbers from the opening,

John accepted a torch that Ted had fashioned from a twisted knot of mesquite. He ducked into the adit and led the way down into the mine. "Lean back and hold on to the side, men," he said. "It's easy to slip and get hurt along here."

The men reached the bottom of the slope without falling, and found what John expected. Bones were scattered over an area of several yards. Three human skulls were unmistakable. Ted Bennett stepped ahead of John and stooped to examine some ragged pieces of cloth and leather mixed in with the bones.

He reached down to pull something from the debris. "Here's your father's watch, Johnny. I'd know it anywhere." He turned to pass the watch back to John. When John took the watch Bennett reached out to take John's arm.

"Let's get out of here, Johnny. We've confirmed that he's here. We can have the undertaker come out and take care of the bodies another day. We'll put the timbers back up to close the opening now and I'll come back down here with the undertaker to show him where to go."

Without speaking, John and the men made their way back up the sloping shaft to exit the mine. Two of the men grabbed the heavy timbers and used the back of a hatchet to pound the boards back in place, closing the opening.

Grimly, John watched the men as they worked on the entrance. They didn't speak, but their faces were filled with anger. He could only feel sorrow. Finally he forced his eyes away and walked slowly back to his horse. His father's death was suddenly real. His chest hurt. As soon as the men finished and mounted their horses, he spurred Prince to a fast trot and guided him out of the scrubby brush around the salt lick to head west. He wanted to hurt someone.

They caught up with the other group of riders waiting in the big pines about ten miles beyond Black Spring. John's face was a mask of anger. His gaze took in the entire group of men. He asked curtly, "Why have you stopped?"

One of the men stepped forward and pointed to his left. "Them rannys are just over the ridge thata way. It musta took 'em a bit of time to gather up the cows. Or else they ain't a bit worried about anybody following them. We figured as long as we had our eye on 'em we was doing what you wanted."

John shook his head. The men had done exactly as he had ordered. He had no call to be angry with them. He looked at the man's face, and recognized him as Tige Conner, a good hand who had shown leadership ability when John had been foreman of the ranch. Conner and his brother had been with the men at the line shack.

Feeling embarrassed and ashamed of the way he had spoken, John said, "Thank you, men, and forgive me for speaking so harshly. We just found my father's bones, and I'm about mad enough to bite nails."

Conner simply nodded in reply, ignoring John's anger. He turned and caught up his horses' reins, waiting for orders.

"What do you think, John. Can we wait until dark and slip up on them?" Ted Bennett asked.

John was thinking fast. He needed these men. If he was to lead them in a shooting fight it was imperative that he have their respect. Taking his anger out on them was no way to show that he would treat them fairly. "That's what I want to do, if these men think that approach will work." He looked over the group of riders as he answered Bennett.

None of the men seemed angry. They had known John was riding to the old mine to search for his father's remains. They expected him to be upset and angry. They all knew they would have been angry themselves under the circumstances, probably violently so.

Conner spoke for the men. "We're ready, Garrett. We all stayed on the Double G and bore up under that skunk Willis and his gun slicks because we rode for either old man Garrett or Tim Hostetter. Both of them was cantankerous as they could be, but they paid good and fed good and treated us decent. We owed them. We figger we got a score to settle with them buzzards same as you."

"Thank you," John said, still looking at the group. "Thank you," he repeated. "I need your help now and I'll need your help getting the ranch back in shape. I hope you will be willing to stay and work for me after we get the cattle back."

Without waiting for the men to answer he continued. "Let's rest here for a couple of hours. That'll give the men pushing the herd time to move along a ways. It wouldn't do to catch them in daylight or before they get well away from Double G land. We'll follow slowly enough to catch up with them around midnight tonight. Most of them will probably be tired and in camp asleep by that time."

"If we stay in the pines we can parallel the trail. Even if they have a lookout on their back trail we won't be seen. Tend to your horses and try to catch a few minutes sleep, men. You won't be getting any tonight."

The sun was going down when John stood up from where he had been resting against the bole of a tree. He led Prince to water then rearranged his bridle. One by one the men followed his lead. They all carefully watered their horses and checked their weapons in preparation for attacking the rustlers.

Once he was mounted, John turned to the cowboys and said, "Ted and Otis and I will move out in front of you men by a couple a hundred yards. When we spot the herd we'll find a good place to tie our horses and go ahead on foot to find their camp. The rest of you hang back and keep quiet until one of us comes back for you. Whoever comes will tell you what we plan to do."

It was dim and quiet under the great trees. There was no sound from the horses' hooves on the bed of pine needles as they walked between the trees. In several places, the brush at the edge of the forest was so thick it forced the riders to move back in the trees too far to watch for the herd, but after about an hour the night began to lighten. Eventually the moon was bright enough for them to find the rustler's camp.

John held up his hand in a signal for the men behind him to stop. He had been hearing cattle for several minutes. It wouldn't do for them to get too close. One of the rustlers riding night guard might hear their approach. He and the two men with him dismounted and tied their horses to a low limb. As the other men drew near, John motioned for them to stay there and wait someone came to get them.

The three men worked their way along to get closer to the herd, staying under the shelter of the trees. Soon Ted motioned to John and Otis to stop and raised his hand to point out the red glow of a spent campfire. The rustlers had made camp in a group of cottonwoods near the creek.

"You and Ted wait here, Johnny," Otis said softly. "I'll fetch the men." Without waiting for discussion, he turned around and disappeared in the gloom.

Minutes later the riders emerged from the darkness and crowded around John. No one spoke. John whispered, "Conner, you take two men and work your way across to their horses. We'll give you ten minutes to get in position. I'd like us to take as many of them prisoner as we possibly can."

"Otis, you take two men and work your way around to the other side of the camp. You get in place and be ready to jump in about ten minutes from now. The rest of us will run across this open space between here and the cottonwoods. When I yell, you come on in too. If we can get close before they realize it I think most of them will give up without shooting."

Conner and Otis were gone as soon as he finished speaking. John took his father's watch out of his pocket, checked the time and placed it on the ground in front of him. The men around him sat on their heels, shifting slightly every few minutes. Finally John touched the man next to him and whispered in his ear, "Get ready to run when I do. Pass the word."

The men stood up and drew their pistols. They crowded close and watched for John to give the signal to move. He checked his watch to make sure they had allowed Conner and Otis enough time to reach their positions. Raising his Colt John stepped out of the shelter of the trees. Taking long, almost running steps, the men were across the open space and at the edge of the camp in seconds.

"You men get your hands up!" John yelled. "You're surrounded. Get your hands in the air or we start shooting."

Men scrambled out of their blankets. One came up shooting. He fell back, riddled with bullets from several guns. The others stood with their hands raised, befuddled with sleep, shock, and surprise. Off to the left they heard two shots. One sounded as though it came from a shotgun.

"Get rope from their gear, men. Tie their hands behind them and we'll tie them on their horses. It's a long way back to Hinton.

Ted walked over to the dead man and began to search his pockets. "You might know Poag Schmidt wouldn't listen to anybody," he said to no one in particular.

"Wait a darn minute. Why in blazes are we going to take these buzzards back to Hinton?" Otis demanded. He moved to stand in front of John with his hands on his hips. "There's a couple of big trees right here in this grove and we've got plenty of rope. These men are rustlers, plain and simple. There ain't no need of dragging them back to town. Shucks, the jail's already full anyway."

"Easy Otis. Take it easy now. I know we used to hang rustlers, but we're not going to hang these. We're taking them to Hinton and turning them over to Del Ketchum and that United States Marshall."

"But, Johnny—"

"Forget about it, Otis. We're taking them in."

"Well, blast," Otis said disgustedly.

Chuckling, John gripped the old man's shoulder. "Thanks for your help, Otis. I know Pa would appreciate it."

"It's nothing, son, if anything I owe you, I haven't had so much fun in donkey's years."

"Hello the camp," Tige Conner called from the edge of the cottonwoods. "I've got a wounded man here."

"Hey, look at that," Ted said as he began to laugh. "Tell us where you're wounded, mister."

The man was leaning forward as though searching for something on the ground and holding his right hip. Conner was holding him by one arm. He led him into the middle of the camp near the fire. As he lay down on the ground on his stomach, groaning loudly, it became apparent that the seat of his pants had been peppered with birdshot. The whole group of cowboys began to laugh boisterously.

Otis leaned toward the man and yelled, "Serves you right, you low-down thief, just sitting in jail is way too good for you."

Conner came over to John and said. "I heard two or three horses running on the other side of the herd just after the shooting was over. I reckon it was the men that were riding night guard sneaking away."

"Don't worry about them, Conner. We've got the majority of the herd back. If they get away, good luck to them. I don't think we'll ever be bothered with them around here anymore. We have more prisoners than enough to worry about anyway. Our job now is to get the herd started back toward the ranch buildings so they can be guarded, and get these men into Hinton.

"Tell the men that since the rustlers are securely tied, I think we should run a rope through their arms and tie them to a couple of trees until we can have some hot coffee and some food. These fellas seem to have more supplies than a wagon train needs. I expect we're entitled to them."

Several men built up the fire and began to cook bacon and boil coffee. Someone found several cans of beans and another the things he needed to make fry bread. Soon the men were eating like hungry wolves.

When the camp was cleaned up and the rustlers securely tied in their saddles, a weary but satisfied group of men headed back to the Double G. Conner took six men and began to push the herd to a pasture closer to the ranch house. John took the rest of the men and led the prisoners along a direct route toward Hinton.

Chapter Eleven

Dawn was breaking when they reached Hinton, but it was still early enough for John and his men to get the their prisoners to the jail without attracting a mob of townspeople. Del Ketchum must have been watching for them through the window of the sheriff's office, because he stepped out on the boardwalk just as John and the others were tying their mounts.

"What in the world am I going to do with this crop?" Ketchum asked, shaking his head. "Garrett, I don't have room for all of these men."

"They'll just have to crowd up in those two cells with the others, Del. We caught them at Black Spring, pushing a bunch of Double G cows toward Smithville," John replied. They had the whole herd off ranch property, and had set night guards around it. If we hadn't gotten there when we did, they would have been in the badlands, and we would probably have never found a cow."

"Are those two men draped over their saddles dead?"

"Er . . . no, only one of them is dead. I expect the one on the roan feels like he is, but he just caught a load of bird shot in his hind parts."

"Well . . . I'll be a son-of-a-gun. You fellas have been busy. Help me get these rannys inside the jail, you men."

"Somebody go fetch the doc," Otis said sarcastically.

181

"He'll probably want you to carry that poor fella on down to his office. It may take him a while to pick out all of that shot he's carrying. We wouldn't want to be responsible for him dying of lead poison, now would we?"

"By the way," Ketchum said, addressing the entire group. "I found out that several of the men we've got in jail here are wanted and there are rewards offered for their capture."

"I'll be willing to bet that even more of these galoots we just brought in will be wanted by the law," John said. "Del, I'd take it as a favor if you would go ahead and apply for the rewards in my name and we can divide the money among all the men who have helped with this fight."

"That's good thinking, John," Del answered, smiling as the group of men nodded in agreement.

"By the way, the marshall and two deputies came in on the stage yesterday. They spelled me so I could sleep some in the evening, and I took over again at midnight. They should be here before too long."

"Have you heard anything from the circuit judge?" John asked. "He's the only one who can clear some of these rannys out your jail."

"He answered my wire and said he'd come here next. I hope he gets here soon," Del said wryly as he opened the office door and motioned for the men to follow him with their prisoners. "This bunch will just have to sit on the floor in the hallway in front of the cells. I'll ask one of the deputies to stand guard on the back steps in case they try to give me any trouble."

"Leave their hands tied. We're going to have enough trouble with this crowd as it is. The marshall will probably want to move some of them to the storeroom in the back of the mercantile or somewhere where they will be more secure. He talked about putting some of them over there yesterday."

After settling the new prisoners in the hallway of the jail, John headed to the hotel to get some sleep. As he walked to the hotel he looked around for Ted, but finally decided he must have gone home while he was talking to Del. Still sick over the events of the day before, John again propped a straight chair under the door handle and fell on the bed to sleep.

It was dark when John woke up. He knew he had slept for a long time. He looked out of the window into the night. The sky was gray to the east. He had slept for hours, almost around the clock. His body was just trying to catch up. No one could go on forever without enough rest.

There was water in the pitcher on the dresser. As he started to pour it in the basin he noticed that there was a thin skim of ice on top. It had turned cold during the night. It was time. Hinton was high up and winter came early.

John took off his shirt and cleaned himself up as much as he possibly could without clean clothes and hot water. He would buy some clothes and get a shave as soon as the town woke up. He felt refreshed when he finished. The sun had risen while he was bathing.

Stepping back to the window, he looked up the street toward the café. They were just lighting the lamps. Surely they would have coffee ready by the time he walked down there. Lights were also on at Ted's place.

"That seems a little strange," John said to himself. "Ted has never been an early riser."

He stared out of the window and thought about the events of the last few days for several moments. Finally he decided to get some breakfast and clean up before he tried to deal with anything. So much had happened in such a short a time. It was hard to get used to the idea that his father was dead. It suddenly came to him that he was the owner of the Double G.

John nodded but did not speak to several people that entered the café as he was waiting for his food. His mind was on the drastic changes in his life. He tried to think about his father's murder, but his mind kept going back Andrea. He asked himself over and over, *Will Andrea be willing to marry me? Will her father even allow me to ask her to marry me?*

He had believed that Andrea made it clear that she cared for him up on the rim after his fight with Willis. Maybe he was wrong to assume such a thing. Suddenly he was struck by the uncomfortable thought that she was probably just grateful to be saved from that brute Willis and he had misunderstood. It was possible.

People were moving along the street when John exited the café. He went to the mercantile and purchased a complete change of clothing and crossed the street to the barbershop. There he got a shave and haircut, then indulged in a hot bath. Dressed in new clothes and really clean for a change, he felt much better. He headed toward Ted's place. He cursed himself for a fool for questioning how Andrea felt toward him. He was sure.

As he walked along the street he saw Ted come out of his door. He was dressed in a suit and wore a hat. He turned away from John without noticing him and entered the stage office. John pulled his father's watch out of his pocket and checked the time. A stage was due in a few minutes. He remembered that Ted had told him earlier that Elaine Hostetter was coming back, and he was going to propose marriage to her. *He must be expecting her on this stage,* He thought. *I wish him luck. There's no telling about women.*

John went back to the hotel and stuffed his dirty clothes in his saddlebags. Gathering them up along with his rifle, he went to the livery to get Prince. The hostler had rubbed the horse down and fed him well. The horse seemed to be glad to see John and as soon his saddle was in place he danced as though he was ready to run.

Leading Prince, John went around the buildings to stand in the alley where he could see the stage come in. He heard it coming just as he reached the edge of the boardwalk. As soon as the stationmaster dropped the step on the side of the stage, a small, slim woman in a dark green travelling costume stepped down to the street. She smiled a little and held out her hand to Ted as he rushed to greet her.

John couldn't hear what she or Ted said, but it didn't look as though she was all that glad to see him. He stepped out of the alley and ground hitched Prince at the end of the station porch. "Hello there, Mrs. Hostetter," he said, removing his hat and holding out his hand as he walked up to the woman. He thought he saw relief in her eyes. *Now why should she be relieved to see me?* he wondered.

"Johnny Garrett, I am glad to see you. My husband always liked you. Thank you for meeting me."

She turned to Ted and said, "It was good to see you, Mr. Bennett, and I appreciate your offer, but Johnny will see me to the hotel. He and I have a lot to talk about. I'll come by your office before I leave town. I believe there are still a few of my husband's papers in your safe and I should have them."

John found it hard to tell if he or Ted was the most astonished at the woman's words. He watched bemused, as Ted tipped his hat and turned to walk back along the boardwalk without speaking.

"Thank you, Johnny," Elaine Hostetter said. "I know Ted Bennett is your friend, and I'm sorry if I offend you, but I have always believed that he knows something about my husband's death. It gives me the willies for him to touch me."

"Does he know you feel that way?" John asked.

"Apparently not; he keeps writing to me. He acts as though I should be grateful that he notices me, the dandy."

Chuckling, John held out his arm. "Let's go. You're probably hungry. I just had the best breakfast in the territory over at the café. The station master will see that your bags get over to the hotel."

"That's fine with me. Walk me to the café if you will, Johnny, then I need a favor. Do you know where Del Ketchum is?"

"Del's acting sheriff. I expect he's in his office."

"Will you go and tell him where I am?" she asked.

"Well, of course I will," John answered. He was astonished at her request. "Here's the café, you go on in and order your food. I'll go to the jail and send Del right on over here."

"Thank you Johnny. We'll explain everything to you later."

John watched her enter the café, then hurried to the sheriff's office. "Del, go get breakfast at the café. There's someone there who wants to see you."

"Someone who wants to see me?" Ketchum asked a little testily. "Can't you tell me who it is?"

"No, but I can tell you this. You won't need your gun or your badge."

"What in the world are you talking about, Johnny?" Del slammed his hand down on his desk in exasperation.

"I'm sorry, Del," John answered. "I need my head checked. Elaine Hostetter is over there eating breakfast and she wants to see you right away. She asked me to send you over."

Ketchum's mouth dropped open and he stared at John for a moment. He carefully took off his badge and unbuckled his gun belt, and without another word he jumped up and raced out of the office door. John could hear his boot heels hitting the boardwalk as he ran down the street to the door of the café.

"Well," he said to himself, shaking his head. "If that don't beat all. I wonder if he's another one of us poor men who have assumed too much about how a woman feels toward him? I hope not. Del's a good man."

John sat in Ketchum's office trying to go over in his mind all the confusing ins and outs of the events of the last few days. He kept asking himself how Ted fit into the mix. He needed to talk to Del and Alec. He would also like to question Elaine Hostetter some. Her statement that she believed Ted had something to do with her husband's death was a shocker.

Del would probably know if Ted had been in on any of the night meetings that Hamilton had with Willis. He remembered that Del had told him that one of the wounded men they brought in from the fight at Blaine's ranch wanted to talk. A fellow named Will Simpson. Maybe he could go to the doctor's place before he left town and talk to the man.

A pounding on the front door of the office yanked John out of his study. He opened the door to find the marshall and one of his deputies standing on the boardwalk. He quickly introduced himself and explained that he was just filling in for Ketchum while the sheriff ate his breakfast. He saw no need to explain to the marshall about Elaine Hostetter.

"I'm Jake Lineacre," the marshall said. "My deputy here is Sim Harris. I moved ten of the prisoners over to that big storeroom in the mercantile yesterday morning. They don't even have to be guarded over there really, but my other deputy is sitting outside the door, just in case."

"Has anyone told you that Willis is dead?" Linacre asked.

"But . . . he was locked up in the jail." John was mystified. "How in heck could that happen?"

"That's a good question." The marshall sat down on the corner of the desk and removed his hat. His hair was iron gray. "All we can figure is that someone sneaked up to the window and dropped a knife inside to the man that did the murder. No one wants to talk about it. The other men claim they didn't see a thing.

"The murderer must have dropped the knife out the cell window after he killed Willis. There was no way to tell who he was. The only chance we have is to make someone talk and I think they're all to afraid for that.

"There's too many men bunched up in the cells. I guess it's possible someone could have killed Willis without anyone noticing. I looked the bunch over and took the ones I thought were the most dangerous over to that storeroom. It's not a very pleasant place. It has a dirt floor, and it smells like cured bacon."

"Do you think the circuit judge will give someone a shorter sentence in return for telling us who killed Willis?" John asked.

"He might," the Marshall answered. "He's tough, and

hates a cattle thief, but he might do that to catch a cold blooded murderer."

"I've been sitting here trying to figure out what's been going on around here. My father's dead. I finally know that much at least. There are far too many cattle on the Double G. Willis had hired all those gunmen to attack Blaine's ranch and drive him out or kill him. He actually had the nerve to try to capture Blaine's daughter. He said he was going to force her to marry him to get his hands on Blaine's ranch, and someone murdered Hostetter a good two years ago. It all goes together and means something, but I can't figure it out."

"I can tell you what's probably the motivation behind this whole mess," Lineacre said. "I found out recently that there's going to be a railroad built down this way. It would pass all the way across Hostetters range just south of that big pond, and catch a corner of the Double G. Whoever owned those two spreads would be able to start a new town near that big spring on the border between the Double G and Hostetter's range. It would make them rich.

"I checked with the bank yesterday. Hamilton was holding a mortgage on your place. With your father dead and you away, nobody knew where, he could have foreclosed and taken over your ranch as legal as you please. I think he had tried it with Hostetter's place and failed. He probably thought that with Hostetter dead his wife wouldn't be able to clear his debts or run his ranch. He didn't allow for the fact that Mrs. Hostetter came from well-to-do folks and had money of her own.

"He also left out of his figuring that she was a friend of Alec Gunnison's. Most folks thought of Alec as just a grizzled old miner who lived up there in the woods. But they figured wrong. Gunnison had taken a whole lot more gold dust out of that hole in the mountain than anyone ever had any idea. He was smart enough to bank it all the way to Smithville, so folks around here wouldn't know his business. Hamilton knew Gunnison had found gold somewhere on Silver Creek Ranch. I don't know how he found out. It could be that he had a friend in the bank at Smithville.

"After Hostetter was killed, Alec and Mrs. Hostetter worked out a deal. I think he just paid the bank the amount of the mortgage and they had an agreement that she would pay him back later, but she had the deed transferred to Alec. He claimed that he was buying it for you."

"Bennett knew all about it, because he drew up the papers," John said, "He told me about it. So I'm not sure of all of the legal ins and outs, but I do know that Alec told me he's planning on riding back to El Paso with those old ranger friends of his and then head on to California like he had planned to before all this mess came up. He'll have to clear all that up for us."

"Is Ted mixed up in the deal somehow?" John asked, hoping the marshall could give him a clear answer. The handwriting on the note he found on Slade's body had bothered him, and he had experienced an uneasy feeling a few days earlier when he saw Hamilton whispering to Ted out in front of the jail, but he still hoped he was clean. When Elaine Hostetter told him that she believed Ted had something to do with her husband's death the uneasy feeling had come back.

"Del Ketchum thinks he is," Marshall Linacre said. "Hamilton would have to have a lawyer to help him get the papers right if he foreclosed on your father's ranch. He would have to have proof of some kind that he had made a real effort to find you before he acted. Ketchum went in the bank one day and saw Ted Bennett and Willis come out of Hamilton's private office together. He said they had their heads together talking when he first saw them, but when they saw he was watching them, they made a show of acting as if they hardly knew each other. They seemed to him to act guilty of something. I do think Willis did all the dirty work. I can't see Bennett or Hamilton shooting anybody unless they were cornered, can you?"

John had dropped his head in his hands as the Marshall spoke. He stood up and began to pace up and down in front of the desk. "I'm having a hard time believing my old friend could have done this. Do you think Bennett or Hamilton ordered Willis to kill my father?"

"I do. There's not much doubt that killing your father so they could take over the Double G was the plan. They probably had no intention of bothering your father until Alec Gunnison and Mrs. Hostetter fooled them on getting her property, but when they couldn't get their hands on that land, they had to have the Double G or they were skunked."

"How do you think they found out about the railroad?" John asked.

"That's what looks so bad for Ted Bennett. He's bound to be the one who told them. He's the only one with connections back east. The telegraph operator says that he gets letters and telegrams from people in Philadelphia almost every week."

"What do you intend to do about him?" John asked, thinking again about the note he found Slade's pocket ordering the killing of the men at the line shack.

"There's not much I can do," Lineacre said, shaking his head. "We don't have any proof that he's done anything wrong. We might be able to prove that he was thick with Hamilton and Willis, but Willis is dead, and Hamilton won't talk. If he tries to point a finger at Bennett he will be branding himself just as guilty as he is."

"Maybe I can get one of the other men to talk," John suggested. "One of the men who were wounded in the fight against Blaine wanted to talk. I don't know if Del got to him yet or not."

"Oh, Ketchum already tried that. He went over to the doc's place to see the man, but he was out of his head with fever, and he finally died before he could tell anybody anything."

"I guess I'll have to go talk to Ted Bennett myself," John said grimly. He dropped his hand to his gun and started for the door.

"Hold it right there now, son. I don't want to have to

lock you up. I don't allow any gunplay in a town I'm responsible for. Just get that notion right out of your head."

John turned to Lineacre, his face showing his anger. "Do we just ignore him then, let him keep on as if he has done nothing? You can't let that happened. My father is dead, and the man who killed him was working with Bennett."

"Bennett doesn't wear a pistol. I noticed that this morning. If you go after him with that Colt I'll have to arrest you." Lineacre stood up and faced John. His face was stern. His eyes bored into John's.

"Let it ride, son. If we get lucky Bennett will just leave town."

"Well, that makes me sick," John complained in disgust. "You're right of course. I can't shoot a man because I think he's done something.

"I'm going out to the ranch. I'll come back to town in a few days. Maybe by then the judge will be here and we'll know something for sure. I can't stay in town. If I do I'll surely run into Bennett, and I don't know what I might do."

Linacre stepped to the little window in the front of the office and watched John as he stood on the boardwalk and talked to Del Ketchum. He couldn't tell the boy, but he planned to see Bennett sometime that day. He would convince him that he would be safer to move to a different town with out delay.

As he stepped out onto the boardwalk, John almost walked into Del Ketchum. The sheriff had a big grin on his face.

"Be the first to congratulate me, John," he said, holding out his right hand. "Elaine just agreed to marry me."

Grabbing Del's hand John shook it as he replied, "That is good news, Del. I do congratulate you. I should congratulate Elaine also. She's a lucky lady."

"I don't know about that. I've loved her for years. She ignored me when Hostetter was alive, but she just told me she feels the same about me as I do about her and she always has. We're planning on getting married as soon as the circuit judge gets here."

"Will you continue as sheriff?"

"Lord no. I hate this job. I hated being a deputy, and trying to be sheriff is ten times worse. I'm a cattleman. Elaine made a deal with Alec to hold her ranch for her until she was ready for it. She's come home to stay. As soon as we're married we're moving out there. We're going to buy some breeding cattle from Blaine and go back to raising cows."

"Well, you can count on me, Del. Come and get me if I can do anything to help you get settled. We'll get together on what to do with the Double G cattle on your range. I'll be pleased to be your neighbor."

"Are you on your way out to Blaine's?"

"What makes you ask that?" John asked.

"I happen to know that Blaine's girl will be eighteen sometime next month," Dell said, smiling broadly.

"Why should I care about that?"

"Maybe you should ride slow and think about it." Ketchum was still grinning as he waved to John and ducked into the door of the sheriff's office.

"Ride slow and think about it, huh—smart aleck," John muttered in disgust as he strode down the boardwalk and caught up Prince's reins. Mounting, he spurred the big horse into a surprised canter right down the middle of the street. As soon as he was clear of the town, he slowed the horse, regretting his bad temper.

Maybe I will go by Blaine's ranch on the way home, he thought. *It would be neighborly for me to check on Bill Blaine's condition and to tell his father what's been happening.*

There was still something he had to do before he could leave town, however. Turning Prince into the field not far from town, John worked his way back to the wooded area that lay just south of the town. He tied the horse in the edge of the woods and walked to the livery barn. Skirting the building along the rear, he stopped to make sure no one was in the alley and quickly crossed the open space to enter the rear door of Bennett's building.

The office door was open. John glanced in and saw that it was empty, and looked abandoned except for several large crates stacked on the floor. He turned back to the stairs, almost automatically removing the rawhide safety loop from his Colt and checking his loads. Settling the pistol against his leg he walked quietly up the steps. As he reached the top of the staircase, Ted came out of the door leading to his rooms and looked down at John.

"I figured you would be here," he said quietly. "Come on in, John. I guess we have some talking to do."

As he followed Ted into the apartment John noticed that there were two crates almost full of books and others that had been nailed shut sitting on one side of the room. "I see you're leaving us," he said, watching Ted intently.

"Yes. I think I've probably outstayed my welcome in this town. I'm sorry, John. I valued our friendship." Bennett walked over to resume packing books into one of the open crates.

John stared at Bennett for a moment, then in a voice that revealed his anger and sadness, he asked, "Were you and I ever really friends, Ted? I didn't think friends plotted to kill their friends fathers or to steal their property."

"You have no proof I had anything to do with any of that. The only thing I've done that can be proven is pass information about the proposed railroad route on to Hamilton and Willis. I admit I would have done more, if they had ever reached that stage. They would have needed me to complete foreclosure and deed transfer papers, but they were so inept they never had that opportunity. The marshall probably knows that much but he can't arrest me for it. Hamilton is the only person who can implicate me and he will never say anything because he knows that if he does it will put a noose around his own neck."

"Sorry, Ted." John pulled a battered-looking piece of paper from his shirt pocket. "I don't need to guess what you might have been in on. I know you were in on everything.

Elaine Hostetter had you figured exactly right. She had a notion or a premonition or something that you were involved in her husband's murder, and she was right. You were in on the murder of Hostetter and the killing of my father. You helped plan the attack on Blaine's ranch as well and I have proof that you were involved. It's right here in your own handwriting."

Bennett's face went ghostly white as he recognized the heavy paper the note John held up was written on. It was the note John had taken from Slade's pocket when the gunman was killed trying to bushwhack the Double G riders at the line shack. Bennett's face contorted with anger. He raised his right hand from the packing crate holding a .44.

John lunged for his Colt. As he was pulling the gun out of the holster the sound of a shot filled the room. Bennett stiffened and stared beyond John, then fell forward against the packing crate without making a sound. John whirled to see Marshall Lineacre standing in the door. He was holstering his Colt.

"I thought I told you I don't allow gunplay in a town I'm responsible for, son." Ignoring John's amazed stare the marshall crossed to Bennett's body and placed his hand against his neck. Satisfied the man was dead, he motioned for John to follow him out of the room. He was silent as he descended the stairs and exited the building. Standing on the last step, he looked back toward John as he pulled the door shut.

"I figured you wouldn't be able to leave Bennett alone. It was plain that somebody with brains was working with Hamilton and Willis, and Bennett was the obvious choice. I reckon I would have felt obliged to face him too if I had been in your place."

"I guess I owe you my life, Marshall. I'd probably be dead now if you hadn't been suspicious enough to follow me. I'm still having trouble believing Ted was standing there holding a gun the whole time we were talking. He would have killed me without a qualm if you hadn't been there."

"He was a snake—a dirty, sneaking snake of a murderer and a thief. He wanted to make a big strike and was willing to do anything to make it happen. Asa Hamilton and Rafe Willis never had the brains to plan out the things they were trying to do. That was always the flaw in Bennett's plotting. If you hadn't found that note in Slade's pocket though, he would have gotten away with it.

"I'll take care of everything here, John. I would like to keep that note Bennett wrote, if you don't mind. You know, son, you should have given it to me when we were talking about this earlier. You took a big chance, and you could have paid for it with your life." He shook his head, holding out his hand for the piece of paper.

John mutely handed the note to the Marshall. He was still in a sort of shocked state. He had thought of Ted as his friend.

"Never mind now," Marshall Lineacre said, reaching out to pat John's shoulder. "It's all over. If I need you to witness what happened here today I'll send somebody out to the Double G to get you."

"Marshall, I thank you again. That seems thin, considering the circumstances, but I can't think of anything else to say. I'll come back to town in a few days. I have to arrange to have my father's body recovered and buried. He'd want a funeral. A lot of his old friends will expect me to do that. I'll need to be here as a witness when the circuit judge gets here to decide what to do with Hamilton and O'Riley and all of their hired men that we corralled in this fiasco."

Thoughtfully John walked across the alley and around the livery barn to the woods. Untying Prince, he mounted and took the road toward the Double G. He barely noticed the road or terrain. His head was full of pictures of Ted Bennett in better days and his father. He kept seeing his father years before, so strong and powerful, and then his body rotting on the floor of an old mine.

When he reached the track down into the valley and Silver Creek Ranch, John stopped and dismounted long enough to remove his coat. The sun had finally warmed him. He stood still for a few moments, gazing at the picture made by the dark cattle scattered over the green grass that covered the floor of the valley made in the bright sunlight. After a while, he shook off the bleak feeling of depression that overtook him every time he thought through the events of the last few days and remounted to started down into the valley, holding the horse to an easy walk.

For the first time in weeks John didn't feel compelled to hurry. He could relax and enjoy the beauty of the wide valley surrounded by towering hills and tall pines. As soon as he reached the level, he pushed Prince to a brisk trot. It was still a fair distance to the ranch house. As he neared the herd, he saw two men running their horses toward him. He stopped Prince and dismounted to wait for them. He didn't blame the riders for being wary, but he didn't want to get shot.

One of the riders was Russ Blaine. He recognized John as he came closer and hailed him. "It's good to see you, boy. Miller here wasn't sure, but I thought I recognized that big red horse of yours." When they reached John both men stayed in the saddle but leaned over and shook his hand in greeting.

"Alec came in last night and told me about your pa," Blaine said. "I'm sorry. It's a heck of a thing for you."

"Thank you, Mr. Blaine. I appreciate it. I'm on my way out to the Double G. I stopped by to find out how your son is doing."

"He's mending, thank goodness. We had almost given him up when it first happened, but my wife's as good with a gunshot wound as any doctor. When the doc came out from town he said there was nothing more he could do for Billy than what she was already doing. He's eating now and sitting up in bed. He'll be all right as soon as he gets his blood built up again.

"Come on up to the house, Johnny. Andrea would probably shoot me if I let you leave without her seeing you. My wife wants to thank you too. She and I are grateful to you for saving Andrea from that skunk Willis. I know we'd have all been done for if you and Alec hadn't helped us stop that bunch of gunmen. Come on to the house and eat supper and tell us what's been happening in town."

John rode beside Blaine to the ranch house. Sandy Miller waved and turned his horse back to stay with the herd. When they reached the yard, Blaine dismounted in front of the barn. "Hey, Jack," he called to a rider sitting in the bunkhouse door. "Put these horses in a stall and rub them down and get them some grain, will you?"

"Don't worry about your horse, John. Jack'll take good care of him. Come on in the house."

Andrea and her mother came out on the back porch as the two men reached the steps. Mrs. Blaine ran down the steps to throw her arms around John. She looked up into his face. There were tears on her cheeks. "God bless you, Johnny Garrett. I don't know what any of us would have done without your help. Andrea told me about O'Riley and Willis. You saved my baby from that awful man."

"Oh . . . please don't upset yourself, Mrs. Blaine," John said, looking toward Andrea and her father for help. He patted Julie Blaine's shoulder awkwardly as she dropped her head against his chest and sobbed.

"Come on now, Julie." Blaine reached over to put his arm around his wife. "John knows we're all grateful. Get on in the kitchen and feed us. That's the best way to show him how thankful you are."

Mrs. Blaine stood back from John and flashed her eyes at her husband. "I'll thank you to bring in a bucket of cold water for supper, Russ Blaine." She turned and re-entered the kitchen, slamming the door.

Andrea laughed merrily. "She sure can put you in your place, can't she, Daddy?"

"Go on with you, girl. You and John have your talk. I'll get the bucket of water and calm your Mama's temper down. We'll call you when supper's ready."

Andrea held out her hand to John. He accepted it in sort of a daze. He and the girl walked hand and hand across the yard to stand at the edge of the trees. John looked at Andrea's profile as they walked. Her nose was perfect. She had her hair lying loose on her shoulders. The edges of soft curls shone like live coals in the sunshine. Her smooth little hand felt tiny clasped in his.

Andrea stopped and looked up at John. "I'm so glad you came. I was almost ready to ride to Hinton myself and find you."

"Would you really have come to town after me?"

"Yes," she answered, still gazing up into his face.

She seemed to be standing closer. John finally could stand it no longer. He reached out and grabbed her by the shoulders.

"Andy, does that mean you'll marry me?"

"Yes, Johnny. Oh yes, I'll marry you," she whispered, slipping her arms up to his shoulders.

Lost in her kisses, John vaguely heard someone calling.

He raised his head and murmured, "I think your folks have noticed what we're doing out here."

"That's all right. I already warned them of what to expect."

John raised his eyebrows and tried to look stern. "Do you mean to tell me you planned this?"

Andrea just smiled and turned away without answering. Holding tight to John's hand, she turned to walk to the house. Russ Blaine stood in the kitchen door and called, "Hey, you lovebirds, come and eat your supper before it gets cold."